The Tales of Fluke & Tash

Ancient Greece Adventure

To

KARA

Happy READING !

M.C.

Fluke and Tash series:

Robin Hood Adventure

Egyptian Adventure

Ancient Greece Adventure

The Tales of Fluke & Tash

Ancient Greece Adventure

MARK ELVY

Available from

www.ypdbooks.com
and
www.flukeandtash.com

© Mark Elvy, 2017

Published by Fluke & Tash Publishing

A CIP catalogue record for this book is available from the British Library.

ISBN 978-0-9934956-6-3

Book layout by Clare Brayshaw

Prepared and printed by:

York Publishing Services Ltd
64 Hallfield Road
Layerthorpe
York YO31 7ZQ

Tel: 01904 431213

Website: www.yps-publishing.co.uk

Greece – Olympia 776 BC...

Herakleitos stopped his early morning work and sat in the shade under his favourite olive tree where the trunk was shaped to fit his body, or, as his wife liked to joke, his body was shaped to fit the trunk. Resting his back against the gnarled branches that had been rooted to the same spot for several hundred years, he unpacked his breakfast of bread, dipped it in some home-pressed olive oil, and began to eat the fruits of his labour as he sat gazing at the stunning scenery stretched out before him. Rummaging in his bag for some cheese, he finished off his breakfast and contemplated getting back to work.

Studying his healthy crop of olives, he noted with satisfaction they were ready for picking, *'It should be a good harvest this year'* he thought to himself. A year's hard work, pruning and tending to his trees, plenty of sunshine and a bit of luck should provide a good crop to take to market. His eyes reached the last visible tree on his small holding farm estate when he was distracted by two voices. He looked on with pride at his two children frolicking around. The twins were racing up the steep hill towards him. Demetrios was his son and heir, the elder by a mere twenty minutes, and was currently winning the race with his younger sister, Appollonia.

Reaching their father's position at the top of the hill, Appollonia said 'It's not fair! You're allowed to compete because you're a boy and I'm not allowed just because I'm a girl. You know I'm as good as you, if not better. I can run faster, jump higher and throw further than you ever can,' she said, shaking her head in frustration.

'I beat you, didn't I?' said her elder brother Demetrios, with a cheeky grin which wound his sister up even more.

'You cheated!' said a perplexed Appollonia. 'You said *wow look at that magic flying object in the distance* and when I turned around you ran off!'

'Now, now you two, no arguing. Demetrios, you've got school shortly, and Appollonia your mother needs a hand at home,' Herakleitos said as he brushed the residual bread crumbs off his clothes and put his bread, cheese and olive oil back in his bag.

The twins began to sulk, Demetrios because he had to go to school, and Appollonia because she would have to wait until the evening for her chance to beat her big brother in another competitive race.

Their father noticed their glum expressions and said 'OK, an extra hour, you can fit a lot of sports into an hour you know.'

'An hour?' said Appollonia eagerly. 'We've got time for some discus, or are you afraid I'll beat you?' she teased her brother.

Herakleitos chuckled to himself, left the twins to argue amongst themselves, and headed off to tend his olives and make preparations for the harvest.

Present Day

The Race is On...

The woods were a peaceful scene of calm and tranquillity. Long-fingered rays of sunlight occasionally penetrated the overhead canopy, lighting the way for the occasional walker. Two such ramblers, day bags fixed firmly over their shoulders, had made their way through the dense woods, enjoying the fresh air that mother nature provides. Birds twittered all round them and the occasional muntjac deer could be spotted if they were quiet enough and didn't startle the skittish creatures. The ramblers were currently stood studying their Ordnance Survey maps – the left path was a quicker route back to their car, or the right path took them a couple of miles out of their way, but midway was a nice local pub serving hearty food and decent real ale. They took out a coin and were just about to spin *heads or tails* to decide which path to take when the peace was shattered by the entrance of Fluke and Tash sat astride their magic case. Flying at some speed, Fluke narrowly managed to miss several tree branches.

'*Duck...*' hollered Fluke at the top of his voice to his passenger, Tash. 'And not the feathered kind either!' He successfully steered and weaved a course through the low-hanging branches of the wooded area, known by Fluke and Tash as *Nummer's Wood*. Their magic suitcase tore through some loose branches and appeared in a small open clearing, and headed at some speed towards the startled ramblers. Fluke himself was taken aback as he didn't notice the two walkers until the last minute, and at the last second the case veered off to the right and drove deeper into the woods, crashing through more branches, causing startled wildlife to flee the surrounding area.

'What was that....?' one of the ramblers asked, turning to his colleague for an answer.

'Beats me...' the other replied, brow furrowed, 'might it have been a U.F.O?' he said, nervously scanning the dark forest for more intruders.

'I don't know about you, but you can forget *heads or tails*, the pub can wait! I'm taking the left path and getting out of here quickly, if you think I'm hanging around to see any more U.F.Os or little creatures flying through the woods you can think again!' And with that they virtually ran down the left path, all the time looking over their shoulders to make sure they weren't being followed.

The magic suitcase was weaving between large tree trunks, and Tash, eyes firmly shut, shrunk as low as she could and held on for dear life, one paw clinging onto the side of their magic suitcase while the other hung onto Fluke's shoulder.

She was beginning to doubt the wisdom of giving Fluke driving lessons, and her doubts were confirmed when one of the *L-plates* she had stuck to the front of the case as a joke was ripped off by a sharp, gnarled tree branch, leaving yet another deep scratch etched into the front, which just added to the collection on their already battered magic suitcase. The case broke free from *Nummer's Wood*, the last branches giving up on their attempt to hold onto the case, and Fluke steered them into clear air, noticeably breathing a huge sigh of relief.

Tash looked over Fluke's shoulder, and gasped. 'I think we're in trouble Fluke.'

'How come? We've got through the trees OK. Alright, we *might* just have picked up a little scratch or two, but no major problems...'

Tash interrupted Fluke midsentence. 'Yep, we've got through the trees OK, but a much bigger problem lays ahead.' Pointing over Fluke's shoulder to a familiar-looking car way off in the distance, she continued, 'That's Mum and Dad's car up ahead, and they got a massive head start on us.'

'Crikey, you're right Tash! We've got to beat them home, can't have them finding us missing or discovering our magic suitcase. They think we're curled up on the sofa snoozing!' and with that the race was on. The main advantage they had over a car was when you're flying you don't have to use roads, so Fluke headed off at a forty-five degree angle, desperately nursing as much speed as possible from the case and hoping to use the shortcut to beat the car in a race home.

Fluke looked over the edge of the case, gazing down from this height on the small postage stamp gardens, chose what he hoped was the right house, and landed the magic case successfully in the garden. The case skidded to a stop, right up against the Nummer's tree stump front door. Hopping off the case, Tash noticed the little front door in the tree stump open wide, and there stood beaming was Papa Nummer.

'Have you been out on another adventure?' he asked Tash, slightly envious of the time travelling adventure trips they seemed to go on.

'What, without consulting you first?' she joked. 'You know we *always* consult you before we go anywhere! No, Fluke has been having driving lessons, but look, we can't chat for long, Dad's car is coming down the road and we've got to get the case packed up before he gets in.'

'We'll pop out and see you later,' Fluke said over his shoulder, dragging the magic case across the patio towards the door and retrieving his spare key, secreted neatly into his collar. Fumbling with the key he eventually opened the door. 'It's my turn to choose our next adventure, and I have some ideas I want to run through with you if that's ok?'

Papa Nummer smiled and agreed to meet up later. Tash followed Fluke, stepping over the threshold and entered the kitchen. Fluke, in his haste, forgot to lock the patio door, and was dragging the case up the stairs when Dad's car was reversing up the drive. The magic suitcase was stored in the spare room's wardrobe, and they both hastily made their way across the landing to their room, leapt up on the sofa and assumed their standard positions. Tash peered out of the window, and noticed Mum and Dad in conversation with one of the neighbours, so thankfully that would have brought them a few extra seconds, but it had been a close run thing.

They heard the key rattle in the front door and in their Mum and Dad came, armed with shopping bags which were then abandoned on the kitchen floor. The familiar sound of the kettle being switched on, followed by Dad's voice shouting up the stairs, 'Come on you two, were home! Come outside for some fresh air, it's a lovely sunny day.'

Making their way down the steep stairs, Fluke heard Dad say to Mum, 'You forgot to lock the door, sweetness, look it's unlocked!' and the patio door swung open. Mum turned around and said, 'don't you *sweetness* me, it's your job to lock up, so *you* forgot to lock it, not me!' and with that a small argument was started.

'Oops!' whispered Fluke grinning, turning to Tash. 'That's my fault, I was in such a hurry to get in I forgot to lock it again.'

'We must be more careful next time,' Tash whispered back, a large grin spreading over her face, and they both went out onto the patio, pretending this was the first time they'd been out today. Fluke flopped down on the warm patio slabs in the sun, whilst Tash favoured one of the garden chairs, yawned and curled up on the comfy chair cushion, both chuckling to each other as the *whose fault* argument raged on in the kitchen.

'He never learns,' said Tash. 'When will he realise Mum *always* wins the arguments. It's a bit like you and me Fluke, you know *I* always win as well!' but Fluke was refusing to be baited and ignored Tash, instead curling up to enjoy the sunshine, and working out what they were going to discuss with Papa Nummer later about their next adventure.

The Olympic Games...?

The afternoon wore on. Mum and Dad had joined Fluke and Tash on the patio, extra deck chairs had been recovered from the garden shed, cushions plumped up, and an hour later Mum was fast asleep. Dad had started to read his book but eventually gave up – it fell off his lap and landed on the floor as he also drifted off into a deep sleep.

Fluke looked expectantly over to Tash and pointed to the Nummer's tree stump. Tash nodded, stretched and jumped down from her chair and joined Fluke as they padded quietly past the now snoring Dad and headed over to it. Fluke knocked at the little wooden door and waited patiently. Seconds later, the door opened and Fluke was met with the smiling face of Papa Nummer and his wife Mama Nummer.

'What's that racket?' Papa Nummer said, looking all round. 'Sounds like someone has a hedge-strimmer going.'

Tash pointed over her shoulder towards the patio, 'Oh that's just Dad snoring; loud though isn't it?!'

Fluke was rubbing his paws together – his excitement was beginning to build as he wanted to get started. 'He'll be asleep for ages, so let's get started.'

'So where are you planning to go for your next adventure?' Papa Nummer asked.

'Ancient Greece!' beamed Fluke turning to Tash, waiting to see her expression. Tash nodded her approval, but kept silent letting Fluke have his say.

Fluke continued, 'We've been watching the usual sports on television and apart from football, cricket and golf, what has been advertised recently? The Olympic Games, the greatest sporting event ever. They've had this documentary about how the Olympics first started, way back in 776 BC. I thought we could go back to the very first Olympic Games! C'mon Tash what do you reckon? It will be fun, just think about it, *pleeeeze*!'

'Ancient Greece and the Olympic games?' smiled Tash. 'Well, you won't have any argument from me Fluke, as that sounds like a great adventure! I'm impressed, you've actually thought about this haven't you? You've even done some homework, looking up the right dates. Well what do you think Papa Nummer, has Fluke *actually* suggested something useful?'

Papa Nummer smiled and asked Mama Nummer to bring out the family tree. They untied the red ribbon, rolled out the parchment and stood round gazing down at the long list of dates. 'Fluke's correct' said Mama Nummer, glancing up and smiling at a chuffed looking Fluke. Her finger had moved down the long list and hovered over 776 BC. 'We had some family in and around Ancient Greece, and they lived in a small village near Olympia.' She moved aside to let Fluke and Tash get a closer look.

'Olympia was an ancient Greek sanctuary in southern Greece. It's located in a *polis* or city, called Elis...' Papa Nummer continued from where his wife left off, 'Sounds like it will be fun, but be very careful...' he said, looking up at Fluke and Tash. 'It was also a dangerous place.'

'Dangerous? Why dangerous?' asked Fluke. 'We can dodge a flying javelin, keep clear of any shot-puts and keep away from any stray discus throwing!'

'I meant the so-called mythical creatures, Fluke.' Papa Nummer looked at them both. 'You had *Medusa,* a hideous-faced creature with a head full of live venomous snakes that turned you to stone; the *Cyclops*, a race of one eyed giants; the *Centaur,* half man, half horse; the *Sirens,* who were beautiful creatures but lured unsuspecting sailors to be shipwrecked on the rocky shores; the

Harpy, a winged creature; the *Gegenees* who were six-armed giants; not to mention your favourite, Fluke, the *Minotaur,* a half man, half bull creature that lived in the centre of the Labyrinth.'

At the mention of a bull, Fluke shivered despite the heat and looked up in dismay, 'Oh no, not bulls again. It will be just my luck to come across one of those creatures! I thought these were mythical, as in not real?' Fluke said nervously.

'Well, maybe they weren't real as nobody really knows, but these legends started somehow and came from somewhere, Fluke – legends don't just start themselves, all I'm saying is be careful.'

Tash agreed. 'We'll be *extra* careful now you've mentioned all those creatures. Great idea Fluke, we'll leave tonight!' and then she stopped, looking around in alarm – the *hedge-strimmer* had stopped. 'Quick, pack up and get inside, Dad's awake! Come on Fluke, let's get back down to the house before he discovers us talking to the Nummers.' They all said hasty goodbyes and packed up their family tree. Both Nummers wished Fluke and Tash an exciting adventure and a safe return, and disappeared back through their little wooden door.

The 12:22 Express...

Fluke was lying next to Tash on the floor, both watching the cuckoo clock intently, willing it to reach "*Bedtime o'clock*" for Mum and Dad. The long lazy afternoon on the patio had made them sleepy, and sure enough when the hands reached 11:30 the television set was switched off by the remote control. Dad stood, yawned, and made his way into the kitchen, and heard Mum say sarcastically 'Don't forget the patio door honey, you can't forget twice in one day.'

'Don't forget the door, honey,' he said, shaking his head as he mimicked Mum's voice. Lights were extinguished and Dad followed Mum, the mini-tiff earlier on in the afternoon was continuing as they climbed the stairs.

'Give it another half hour, Fluke,' said Tash smiling, 'because as usual Dad will attempt to read and is bound to fall asleep shortly'.

Sure enough, bang on 12 o'clock gentle snoring could be heard from the bedroom and at the same time the doors on the cuckoo clock sprang open, releasing the little wooden bird, who flew out for a few seconds of freedom to let everybody know midnight was here, before the spring dragged it back inside the clock.

'Ready?' asked Tash and watched Fluke jump up, eager to be off.

He beamed a huge smile, 'Ready? Of course I'm ready! C'mon let's get the case out and head off,' he whispered over his shoulder as the pair tiptoed carefully up the stairs, across the landing and into the spare room.

'After you...' Tash stood back and watched as the wardrobe doors were opened, 'and you're driving today,' she whispered.

Fluke reached inside and moved coat hangers along the rail to get better access and eagerly took out their magic case. Placing it on the floor, he opened the lid, took out the booklet and sat on the floor studying its contents, flipping through it until he found the page he wanted.

'Aha, found it!' exclaimed Fluke with a grin. Reaching over he set the coordinates on the case, waited a few seconds and rummaged deep inside, keen to see what outfits the case would provide.

Putting his new costume on, Fluke studied himself in the wardrobe door mirror. Tash retrieved her costume and stood side by side with Fluke – both outfits were similar. Tash's consisted of some woollen cloth folded and pinned together, with holes for the head and arms. It was called a *peplos*. Fluke meanwhile wore a plain woollen tunic which was tied at the waist. The case had also provided a pair of similar looking cloaks called *himations*, which Tash stored back inside the case should they need to wear these later.

Closing the case lid, they both leapt on and, with a final check of the coordinates, Fluke looked around the room, his eyes resting on the red glow from the digital clock as he noted the time of 12:22, their normal departure time.

'All aboard the 12:22 express...' he joked with Tash. 'Make sure you fasten your seatbelts and your tables are in the upright position – next stop ancient Greece. Are you ready?' he asked eagerly.

'I'm ready, Captain Fluke,' Tash said between fits of giggles, 'this is going to be one exciting adventure!' She watched as Fluke turned the handle three times. The case began to spin, and the wind picked up, which caused Fluke's ears to flap, and the case promptly vanished from the spare room.

776 BC

The Olive Tree...

Within seconds, night-time back home had turned into a bright sunny morning, the sunlight was dazzling. Fluke sat up front gazing around at the scenery, enjoying every second of the short flight, but knowing very soon he would have to negotiate a safe landing somewhere below. Tash, sat behind, was looking down below at the breath-taking coastline they were currently flying over, and up ahead was a beautiful landscape of hills and olive trees. The case began its descent, the tops of the olive trees were getting closer with each passing second.

'We need to find a clearing soon, Fluke,' she hollered over the wind into Fluke's ear, and the pair began a scan of the ground below. They spotted a small clearing between rows and rows of the trees. Fluke was concentrating hard, circling above whilst getting lower with each pass, wrestling with the steering trying to line up their case. Neither noticed two people below and were both astounded to suddenly witness a disc-like object heading straight for them. The disc struck the front of their case and spun off.

The collision with the mysterious object had caused their case to spin wildly out of control and they were now heading towards a large olive tree. The steering wasn't responding and Fluke let go of the case and covered his face with his paws, whilst Tash looked over his shoulder and gasped an 'Oops' as realisation dawned on her exactly where they were going to end up.

There was an eerie silence as the case came to a shuddering halt and became firmly wedged in the tree branches. Tash was balanced precariously on a tree branch, hanging onto the suitcase handle. She looked around for Fluke. He was just below her, albeit hanging upside down, and he appeared to be relatively unscathed, his new woollen tunic caught on a tree branch which had stopped him from falling.

'What is it with you and trees, Fluke?'

'I don't know what you mean,' he replied rather defensively.

'You've got a short memory – how could you possibly forget the tripwire and net in Sherwood Forest. If I remember correctly we were upside down in that tree as well!'

'Well yes, we were, *but* look how that turned out, we had a great time!'

'We did once we got down. I don't think Robin Hood is around to help us out of this predicament; were going to have to work this one out ourselves.' She began studying the tree in more detail.

'Errrr... Yuck, that's bitter!' mumbled Fluke between mouthfuls of food.

'Are you eating again? Tash said in near disbelief, 'I can't believe you're thinking about food whilst we're stuck in this tree! What exactly are you chomping on now?' she asked.

'An olive, Tash. It was dangling right in front of my face and let me tell you it tastes nothing like the ones at home!' He stretched out his paw to grab another nearby olive, just in case the first one was off, firstly discarding the olive stone before popping a fresh olive in his mouth. 'Anyway...' he grimaced as the bitter aftertaste kicked in again, 'I thought cats could climb trees?'

'Cats *can* climb trees Fluke, but I don't think dogs are any good, and how are we going to get the case down?'

Fluke paused, unsure what to do with the bitter tasting food, decided to grin and bear it and swallowed the horrid tasting mouthful. Discreetly discarding the olive stone he contemplated Tash's last comment and said, 'We'll find a way Tash, we always do.'

The Trampoline...

Fluke stopped his mini-harvest of the olives, his paws full of the dark green vegetables, *or are they a fruit?* he thought to himself. Looking upwards he mischievously offered a pawful to Tash, chuckling to himself, knowing she would hate the bitter aftertaste.

She ignored the offering and was trying to work out how they were going to climb down from their current predicament when they were interrupted by two soft voices sniggering and whispering to each other. Looking down from her lofty position, Tash saw the source; two children who appeared to be twins by the looks of it, a brother and sister.

'Hi there.' Tash quickly let go of one tree branch with her paw and attempted a wave. 'I don't suppose you can help us get down?' she asked in a kindly fashion. 'It's just that were kind of stuck up here!' and rapidly took hold of the branch again as she nearly fell.

Fluke, upside down, gazed down at the twins and introduced themselves. 'Hiya, I'm Fluke and this...' he pointed upwards, 'is Tash, and if you can help us get down it would be greatly appreciated as I'm getting rather dizzy hanging upside down!' *I don't know how bats do this all day* he thought to himself.

'Told you I saw a magic flying object, but you wouldn't believe me,' Demetrios said poking his sister.

'Well, you normally tell lies so why should I believe anything you say,' Appollonia whispered, her gaze returning to Fluke and Tash, still wedged in the branches of their father's olive tree. Their hushed conversation was interrupted by a shadow that came from behind, turning around Appollonia said 'Dad, it looks like we've got visitors,' and pointed up.

'Well, well, how did you two manage to get up there, *and* hang upside down as well?' said Herakleitos. 'I wasn't going to start olive picking until tomorrow, but I notice that you've already made a start!' he joked with Fluke, indicating the pawful of olives that he'd been eating. 'We better get you down, and I think I have an idea how.'

Issuing instructions to his two children, Herakleitos rummaged in his large bag. Removing his breakfast he delved deeper inside and withdrew a large blanket he normally used to catch the olives that fell from the tree during harvest time. Taking one side all to himself his two children stood side by side on the opposite side of the blanket and all three began walking backwards stretching the blanket as far is would go.

Looking down from their vantage point at the activity taking place below, Tash said, 'Well, I take it you can you see what they're doing and what we have to do next?'

'I really don't have much choice in seeing what's happening below Tash, you seem to forget I'm hanging upside down!'

'If you've not been on a trampoline before Fluke, you're in for a treat.'

Herakleitos checked his two children were ready, looked up and explained, 'just let go of the branches and jump, we'll catch you in the blanket on your way down, just make sure you don't jump both together.'

Tash was the first to let go of her branch and dropped like a stone, passing Fluke on her way down. She hit the blanket, which thankfully took her weight, and was catapulted back up towards the tree again.

As she headed up, she passed Fluke on his way down and they managed a quick high-five when they met in mid-air. Fluke hit the blanket and he too was thrown back up, passing Tash on her final way down again.

'Grab the case, Fluke!' she hollered as they passed each other.

As Fluke reached the tree he reached out, grabbed the handle of their magic suitcase, tugged it free, and it joined him on his downward journey. Fluke hit the blanket for the final time and sat side by side with Tash who was grinning like the Cheshire Cat in *Alice's Adventures in Wonderland*.

The blanket was lowered carefully to the ground. Tash dusted herself down, thanking all three for their help. Fluke meanwhile looked up as a few stray olives fell from the branches and bounced of his head, coming to rest on the blanket beside him.

Found It...

'So tell me...' Herakleitos said jovially, 'now you're back on solid ground, what exactly are a dog and cat doing hanging around in my olive trees?'

'Yes, sorry about that, but Fluke here...' Tash looked over her shoulder to locate Fluke who had wandered off searching the nearby ground, 'is new to driving and something hit us causing our case to spin out of control,' Tash explained, wondering what exactly Fluke was up to.

'Found it!' Fluke exclaimed. He bent down, retrieved whatever it was he was looking for and walked back over to join the group.

'Found what?' enquired Tash, studying the stone disc-like object that Fluke was carrying.

'I found the discus that hit our magic suitcase – well I assume that's what it is?' he shrugged as he handed over the object to Appollonia, who rather shyly took the discus and thanked Fluke.

Introductions were made all round. Fluke and Tash explained about their visit to Olympia, told them a little bit about their magic time-travelling suitcase, and that they were here to watch the forthcoming Olympic Games. The twins were hanging onto their every word, especially when they were told about the magic case, and they both kept glancing at it in awe.

Herakleitos introduced himself and his two children and said proudly, 'Demetrios here is representing our local village in the games, aren't you son?' embarrassing the poor boy by ruffling his hair as parents always seemed to do in public, 'and this is my youngest, my lovely daughter Appollonia, who takes after her mother. Very feisty, hot-headed and has a sharp tongue, so beware!' he joked.

'Yeah, who would just love to compete in the Games as well…' said Appollonia, the frustration evident in her voice, 'but because *she's only a girl* is not allowed, it's not fair'.

'I told you she was hot-headed,' said a laughing Herakleitos.

'So anyway, who threw the discus at us?' asked Fluke.

'Well it wasn't me, it was him…' Appollonia said pointing to her brother, 'because *my* throw would have been a lot further, a lot higher and would have missed you completely!' It was Appollonia's turn to tease her brother, who took it in good jest – their harmless sibling rivalry was obvious. Their father stepped in before the argument got out of control.

'Enough...' he said grinning. His pride in his two children was obvious. 'Demetrios, off to school with you and no arguing. Appollonia, you've got to go home and help your mother around the house; the *who can throw the furthest*, and *who can run the quickest* debate can be continued later on after school and chores.'

'Can't we stay a bit longer dad?' pleaded Demetrios. 'We'd like to talk to Fluke and Tash a bit more, they sound like fun!' He turned to his sister for support, but before she could back her brother up, their father stopped them.

'If Fluke and Tash would like to stay tonight...?' He looked over for confirmation.

'We'd love to, if that's OK with you all...' Tash said eagerly 'and we can tell you some more stories about our magic suitcase'.

'Wow, thanks for the offer...' added Fluke, 'and maybe in the morning before school you can show us both how to throw a discus as well?'

The twins agreed eagerly. 'See you later,' they both said together.

'That's settled then...' said Herakleitos, 'you can all catch up later, *after* school and *after* chores!' and with that Appollonia and Demetrios trudged off together, happy with the promise of more stories to come and even better, more discus throwing before school and chores as well.

Harvest Time...

Herakleitos watched his two departing children walk off – every now and then they both turned around and waved to Fluke and Tash, before they disappeared from sight.

'Well, you two have certainly made an impression, they've really taken a shine to you both. So, now the twins are out of earshot, you can tell me honestly – this case of yours...' he stood studying the battered looking contraption laying on the ground at Tash paws, '... isn't magic and doesn't really fly, does it? Demetrios was mistaken when he said he thought he saw a flying object, I mean there's no such thing as magic, right? Only the twelve Olympian gods have magical powers,' he gazed north towards the direction of Mount Olympus, several hundred miles away.

'Well, no, a suitcase doesn't normally fly, agreed...' Tash looked up at Herakleitos, 'but this isn't your average suitcase either'.

Fluke bent down, fiddled with the case and said 'we'll have to show him Tash, it's the only way,' and, grinning, they both hopped on board.

The case had been set to manual and not the special time travel mode, and it lifted off the ground, hovering directly in front of a stunned looking Herakleitos.

'What...? Why...? How did you...? It can't possibly fly!' He eventually managed to string together a coherent sentence, obviously still flabbergasted. He shook his head in wonderment.

'Harvesting problems are a thing of the past, Herakleitos. We'll give you a hand picking the olives as a repayment for you letting us stay with your family,' Tash said as the case hovered near the top of the tree. She leant over to help Fluke pick the dark green olives, and continued, 'You can concentrate on the lower branches and we'll work from the top down and meet in the middle.'

The blanket they had used as a trampoline, now fully stretched out on the floor, was full of the bitter tasting olives as the tree was gradually being plucked clean by the two new budding farm hands. Herakleitos explained that olives used for eating needed to be soaked in a brine solution for at least twelve months to soften the flavour and remove the bitter aftertaste, as they were way too bitter to eat directly from the tree, which caused Tash to laugh at Fluke's expense. 'See Fluke, you just need to wait a few months before you can eat them.'

As the three grafted away picking, Tash and Fluke were asking a few questions about farming and how they made the wondrous olive oil. It was explained to them about the process of crushing olives between large stones. Oil that was released from this process was caught in clay pots and stored to sell at the markets.

Herakleitos made several trips back and forth to his farmhouse, and each time he brought back some large baskets which were then filled with olives. It was a long day in the field, but both Fluke and Tash were enjoying themselves, guiding the hovering case up and down and then moving from tree to tree until Herakleitos called it a day.

'Time to head back home...' He stopped work, wiped his brow and surveyed their handiwork. Impressed with the volume of olives they had collected in just one day, he continued, 'I'll introduce you to my wife, although Philomela already knows you're staying as when I went home to collect the baskets the twins had already mentioned it! So, who's hungry?'

Fluke's paw shot straight into the air. 'Just a little bit peckish,' he confirmed with a grin, 'I'm not that struck on these olives mind you!' His facial expression wrinkled at the thought of another bitter aftertaste.

'You must try some seasoned olives, Fluke, they've been resting in our special brine solution for twelve months and are perfect for eating, trust me,' Herakleitos said with a huge smile. The trio strolled off into the sunset, heading back to the farmhouse with Fluke carrying the case. They'd left their harvest of olives in the baskets under the trees, the backbreaking task of transporting the olive baskets over to the stone presses would start tomorrow, when Herakleitos would call in a few favours from his fellow villagers to join in and give a helping hand. Village life was like that, everybody mucked in at harvest time and helped each other.

Secret Midnight Meeting...

It was late in the evening and a secret meeting had been hastily arranged in the neighbouring village. This meeting was held when the rest of the village was asleep. A small fire in the *agora* or main village square burnt brightly, shadowy figures of the village elders sat around the edge in discussions awaiting the late arrival of the final member of this secretive group.

Punctual timekeeping at these meetings was expected, in fact demanded. Being late was not an option, however nobody dared to question the late arrival of their final member, the leader of this secret group. They could be as late as they wanted.

Nobody knew the true identity of their leader, rumours were rife, but these rumours were whispered as nobody dare ask for confirmation. Dancing flames cast eerie shadows on the floor, the assembled guests were transfixed by the shapes and sounds the flames and burning logs made, when they were brought out of their trance-like state by a huge hooded figure who had been watching from the dark side-lines, and, when satisfied of not being watched, stealthily crept up on the group and took a seat.

Helios, the village leader, stood, bowed and welcomed their new guest. He was secretly hoping for, but not expecting, a return comment. He wasn't surprised when he didn't get a reply. The hooded figure sat silently staring intently at Helios, causing him to feel nervous and awkward. He hastily sat back down and flanked by his two right hand men, Isandros and Lycus, started the meeting...

How to Throw a Discus...

The family sat round the breakfast table, fully content. Farming was hard work and built up your appetite. Fluke had to admit he now officially loved olives, and the goat's cheese, breads, fish and vegetables that accompanied their dinner the previous night was wholesome and very, very tasty. Breakfast consisted of barley bread dipped in watered-down wine followed by lovely sweet figs.

The day before had been very productive. A good day's harvest was waiting for the stone presses this morning, and helpers from the village had been organised for this once-a-year task. Today was Demetrios's last day at school for a whole week, so he can concentrate on putting the finishing touches to his Olympic training. Appollonia had been up extra early and had already finished her chores with her mother and was eager to get outside and teach Fluke and Tash how to throw a discus.

Whilst they rested after breakfast, Tash led some more storytelling with input from Fluke. They tried to explain as best they could about their magic suitcase. Fluke was in full swing telling everybody about their Robin Hood adventure and how they rescued Marion, whilst Tash concentrated on telling everybody about Ramesses II and their great chariot battle. Raised eyebrows and the occasional gasp came from the twins, which made Herakleitos's wife Philomela lean over, smile and whisper to her husband, 'The twins are enjoying themselves, it's taken some of the pressure off Demetrios and his training, they both look so relaxed.'

The twins were eager to impress their new guests and begged their mum if they could leave the table and do dome more training outdoors.

'Take it easy with them and don't bore Fluke and Tash too much...' she said whilst clearing the table. 'I don't want them to think that's all we do round here – olive farming and sports!'

'Well it is isn't it?' Appollonia said truthfully over her shoulder as she followed her brother through the door, closely followed by Fluke and Tash.

'Oh I just wish she could compete alongside her brother...' Philomela said, turning to her husband, 'she's so competitive and could easily beat most of the boys in the neighbouring villages. It's such a stupid old-fashioned law about boys only competing.'

'I know, I know,' Herakleitos agreed and put his hands up in mock surrender, 'she could beat most people we both know that, but it's the law,' and he helped his wife clear the table.

Once outside, Demetrios had them line up alongside the mud brick and plaster whitewashed wall to the front of their house, 'First thing we need to do...' he explained, eyeing up Fluke and Tash, 'is some light stretching exercises to limber up and get the muscles working,' and promptly dropped to the floor and started a few push-ups, sit-ups, touching toes and running on the spot. Appollonia followed her brothers lead and was keeping pace, everything her brother did she did just as well. Fully warmed up, Appollonia disappeared for a few seconds to a small lean-to building that was built on the side of the property, and could be heard rummaging around inside when a triumphant 'here you are,' filtered back outside.

Clutching the now familiar discus, she also carried a long wooden javelin. Passing them to her brother, he laid the javelin on the ground as a marker, a reference point to take the measurement from on how far they'd all thrown.

'Watch Demetrios demonstrate on how to hold and throw the discus and then watch me teach you how to throw properly!' Appollonia laughed and joked with her brother.

They all stood watching. Demetrios ignored his sister's comments and stood with his feet shoulder-width apart and facing in the general direction that he intended to aim his throw, with his left foot positioned slightly ahead of his right. His upper body was slightly twisted to the right and bent slightly forward at the waist, with his right arm hanging by his side clutching the stone discus, he began to swing the arm back and forth gaining momentum. When he was satisfied, he straightened and twisted his body back round like a coiled spring, at the same time releasing the flattened stone discus, which hurtled through the air gaining height and landed in a cloud of dust, burying itself in the ground around 150 feet away.

Fluke and Tash applauded and watched as Appollonia marked the spot and retrieved the discus. Moving her brother out of the way, she assumed a slightly different pose from her brother, side on, with her feet facing ninety degrees away from the direction she wanted to throw. Going through the same basic routine, right arm swinging back and forth, she swung her upper body through a ninety degree turn whipping her right arm around and releasing the discus it hurtled through the air with incredible speed and landed ten feet further ahead of her brother's throw.

'Crikey, they certainly throw a long way...' whispered Tash, 'And that stone discus looks heavy as well. I think it's your turn next Fluke,' and as she stepped aside to watch she laughed, 'and don't drop it, your paws seem to attract danger – remember Egypt?'

Not Quite an
Olympic Record...

Fluke padded forward and gratefully accepted the flat stone, turned it over and studied it carefully, and commented, 'no wonder this knocked our case off course, it's really heavy!' He stood gazing down the makeshift athletics' field, pretending he was in a huge arena with thousands of spectators watching, and proceeded to swing his paw back and forth building up the momentum, careful to avoid dropping it on his paw as Tash had joked. Just before he released the stone, his left paw slipped on the wooden javelin that Demetrios had left lying on the ground, causing Fluke to stumble and fall backwards. Panicked, he released the discus, which dropped on the floor and rolled some two feet away over the start line.

Tash giggled and walked over to stand alongside Fluke. She put her paw up to her eyes to ease the glare from the bright early morning sunshine and stared down the field, sarcastically searching way off in the distance. 'Did you bring any binoculars, Fluke? You must have thrown it that far I can't see it anywhere, it *must* be a new Olympic record!'

'Yeah, well I guess it's not quite up to Olympic standard, but that throw *might* be a new record for the worst throw in the history of discus throwing,' he grumbled as he bent down to retrieve the stone and passed it to Tash for her go.

'Well at least you didn't have to walk too far to retrieve it,' Tash joked.

Seeing the funny side and forgetting his embarrassment, he laughed 'OK, so it's not the best, but let's just see how you get on shall we?'

Tash strode up and stood behind the line made by the javelin, and took careful aim. Standing side-on as she had watched Appollonia, discus in her paw, she started the same paw swinging motion the others had done, when out of nowhere a big bumble bee on its way back from the fields started buzzing around Tash's head completely distracting her. She flapped her free paw around trying to shoo the bee away with little or no success, in fact it made the bee more determined to investigate Tash more closely. Not wishing to be stung, she tried flapping with both arms to see if that worked, which it didn't. The bee disappeared behind her, and turning around to follow, she started spinning on the spot chasing the bee around in circles. Around and around she went, three or four times at least, each turn she got faster and faster, and desperate to escape the bee she released the stone discus and ran for the cover of the lean-to building.

A few seconds later, realising the bee must have got bored and flown off to bother someone else, she emerged from the building to see all three stood far off in the distance in deep discussions. Heading over, she noticed they were all staring at Tash in stunned silence.

'What? What's happened? Why are you all staring at me like that?'

'Come and take a look...' grinned Fluke. 'If you turn professional and need a manager just let me know will you,' and stepped aside to let Tash see what all the fuss was about. There on the floor, at least twenty feet further than Appollonia's marker was the discus thrown by Tash.

'That's a pretty good throw, no let's be honest here, that's an *amazing* throw,' exclaimed Demetrios, 'it must be good if you beat my sister, as nobody and I mean *nobody* has ever beaten her before!'

'Luck, pure luck, I was just trying to escape being stung by the bee that was buzzing around my head,' Tash said, almost in apology for beating Appollonia.

'Luck it may be...' said Appollonia thoughtfully, 'but I think you've just developed a new technique.

If you spin around a few times, build up speed and momentum, the trick is obviously trying to control when you release it...' she said more to herself than anybody else. She retrieved the discus and walked back to the starting position, muttering to herself, her voice trailed off as she got further away.

'What did she say?' asked Fluke.

'Oh she's lost me...' said Demetrios with a grin, 'that's Appollonia's brain ticking away, always trying to find new ingenious ways of improving her throwing technique and distance, anything to get better and better and stay ahead of me!'

No Dad, You Can't...

The morning sun shone just as brightly in the neighbouring village. Remnants of the fire from the late night meeting were smouldering, all but extinguished, just a few glowing embers remained.

Helios shuffled through the village, flanked as always by his two devious colleagues. He was trying to keep himself busy, not really looking forward to the task they had been instructed to carry out later today.

Isandros broke the silence first, 'That man scares me...' he shuddered, 'I can only imagine his hideous face hidden behind that hood he always wears. Do you think his face is as terrifying as the rumours would have you believe?'

Lycus nudged his fellow colleague nervously, 'Don't mention that man, he gives me sleepless nights. Do you really think he's the messenger and servant of Hades, the God of the underworld as everybody suspects?'

They stopped walking and stood with their backs to a house.

'Enough. We'll not mention this in public,' commanded Helios sternly. 'We do as instructed, nothing more, nothing less. You both know we don't dare question the *Hood*,' the nickname they'd all given the secrctive figure.

'So all we do is kidnap the child on his way back from school and deliver him to the *Hood*?' blabbed Isandros, ignoring the command to not mention last night's secret gathering.

'Yes Isandros,' sighed Helios, 'you were at the meeting last night, or were you asleep when we got our instructions? I'm as uncomfortable with this as you two, but when the *Hood* tells us to carry out a task we just get on with it'.

'Well at least our village will now be one of the favourites to win the *diaulos* foot race,' Isandros chuckled, glancing at Helios. 'I mean surely your son Penthylos can't be beaten now we're going to kidnap his main competition from the village over the hill.'

'No Dad, you can't' cried a voice behind them.

All three spun round to locate the source of the sobbing coming from an open window in the house behind. There, with tears streaming down her pretty face, was Xene, Helios's daughter.

Turning to Isandros, Helios muttered angrily, 'I told you not to mention this in public.'

'Err, we'll meet up later as arranged,' Isandros said sheepishly and practically dragged his fellow conspirator Lycus away, leaving Helios to deal with his distraught daughter.

Helios watched as the pair bustled off and turned to face his daughter.

'What are you doing in there Xene, that's not our house?'

Xene came out onto the street and stood staring sadly at her father. 'Mum sent me over to help out, you know poor old Egina is not well, and don't change the subject, what are you planning, I thought I heard you talking about kidnapping somebody?'

'You're mistaken my girl, and where are you manners? You know you don't question your parents and certainly not in public. Now be off with you, go home to your mother and forget what you *think* you might have heard.'

Helios watched guiltily as Xene looked to argue back, thought better of it and disappeared from view. 'We've got to be more careful....' he whispered to himself. 'Nothing can get in the way of our plans.'

The Mysterious Cloud...

'Come on, last day at school remember?' Herakleitos said as he interrupted the discus training. 'You'll have plenty of time tomorrow and for the next week to train as much as you like.'

'Yes, and he's going to need it!' joked Appollonia.

Demetrios looked crestfallen. 'OK, dad. We were having so much fun I forgot about school,' he said, and reluctantly helped his sister pack away their training equipment, scurried home to change and hurried off to school, already looking forward to home time.

'I've finished all my chores dad, so can I spend the day with Fluke and Tash? I can show them around and take them out to the countryside whilst you do your work.'

Herakleitos looked at Fluke and Tash. 'That might be a good idea, that's if you want to have a guided tour? We have some lovely temples to explore and as I'll be busy pressing olives all day it will keep you entertained.'

It was agreed, a day sightseeing would be nice, so whilst Herakleitos busied himself preparing the stone presses, Appollonia started to come up with some suggested places they could visit.

'How would you like a bird's-eye view of the countryside?' Fluke asked.

'You mean a trip on your magic case?' grinned Appollonia not sure whether she had interpreted Fluke's question correctly.

'Well, we can cram a lot more into the day, you'll enjoy the flight...' Tash confirmed, 'and it might be fun as well'.

'As long as we steer clear of any olive trees,' Appollonia giggled.

'I'll be driving this time so no need to worry about that,' laughed Tash as they headed into the house to retrieve the case.

'It wasn't my fault,' mumbled Fluke feebly.

'Mum, I'm taking Fluke and Tash out for the day to show them around and they said I could go on their magic case.'

Philomela looked slightly concerned and had some doubts. 'Are you sure it's safe to be flying around?'

'Oh, mum it will be fine, besides Tash is driving so we won't be crashing into any trees.' Turning to Fluke she winked at him, letting him know she was only teasing.

They dragged the case outside, gathered around and waited patiently for Tash to set the controls. Satisfied, they all hopped on board; Tash at the front, Appollonia safely in the middle and Fluke sat snuggly at the back.

'See you later.' Appollonia whooped with glee as the magic case lifted off the ground, circled around the pottery tiled roof of her parent's house and headed off in the direction of the hills. Tash expertly guided them over the top of the olive trees and they all waved to Herakleitos toiling below with his fellow villagers bringing in the harvest.

Fluke tapped Appollonia on her shoulder and said above the sound of the wind, 'Are you OK with heights?'

'I think so Fluke...' she laughed and hung on tight as the case banked to the left and headed off towards a rocky outcrop with an old looking stone temple. 'I've never been *this* high before so I wasn't sure whether to be afraid or not!'

Appollonia was clearly enjoying herself and gave them a constant running commentary of each and every temple and village they passed, until they flew over a small village below, similar in size to her own, when she noticeably shivered.

'Are you cold?' asked a concerned Tash from the front.

'No, I've just had a horrible feeling that something bad is going to happen, and whatever it is will happen from that village below,' she pointed downwards.

'Are they enemies of yours?'

'Not really, no. My brother's girlfriend lives there, although he's *sooo* occupied with the Olympic Games he can't see the obvious, that Xene is in love with him, typical boy! Her father doesn't like Demetrios much, feels he's not good enough for his daughter as he's just a farm boy which has caused arguments with my dad,' she laughed nervously. She continued staring down as they passed over the village, the nagging feeling that something bad was going to happen wouldn't leave her until they left the village behind.

They flew on passing places of interest when suddenly their case started to shudder uncontrollably.

'Hang on tight...' requested Tash wrestling with the steering, 'we seem to be struggling with some air turbulence, so if we had seat belts I'd ask you to fasten them securely,' she tried to make a joke.

'That's a weird purple cloud...' said Appollonia pointing directly ahead, 'I've never seen one like that before,' and they all stared at the large cloud of fog that was getting closer. A storm was brewing from within. Flashes of lightning erupted from its centre, closely followed by a noisy clap of thunder.

'Better steer away from it, Tash,' said Fluke nervously.

'I'm trying Fluke, but the case won't respond,' said Tash fighting with the controls. 'Whatever it is, it's dragging us closer, I've lost all steering!' she exclaimed.

'Horrible isn't it when you can't steer!' Fluke half-heartedly joked about his experience yesterday.

Tash, trying to remain calm, gave up fighting the steering as she had completely lost control. Turning round she said, 'I can't change course, the steering's not working at all. It's almost as if the cloud has locked on to us and is dragging us in.'

'It's what's inside that worries me, and how can a cloud drag us in?' Fluke queried apprehensively.

They fast approached the wispy outer fringes. The cloud was getting thicker and the fog seemed to be alive. Long ghost-like fingers of the purple haze surrounded them and seemed to beckon them in. Fluke watched from the rear as the front of the case went in deeper. Tash was the first to disappear into the fog, followed by Appollonia and then Fluke. The case had been swallowed up and had completely vanished from sight.

The Walk Home...

Demetrios was happy. School had finished for the summer break, in fact the whole of Greece had agreed to what they called an Olympic Truce which allowed athletes from all over to travel to the games in safety. The event was going to be a huge celebration, with competing villages all desperate for the honour bestowed on the victorious athletes – their feats would be listed for future generations to marvel at.

The large group leaving school heading home had thinned, people heading off in different directions to their local villages, friends whishing each other luck in the upcoming games, until it was only Coroebus, Demetrios's best friend and training partner, who was left walking alongside.

'So how do you rate your chances in the *diaulos* foot race?' asked Coroebus.

'Not sure. I know Penthylos is competing and he's desperate to beat me.'

'Oh don't worry about him, you know your faster, you've just got to believe in yourself and not worry about anybody else.'

'That's easy for you to say, you know you're the best, I mean nobody's going to beat you in the *stadion* race, you run like the wind. People often joke that you must be the son of Iris, messenger for the Olympian Gods, who travels with the speed of wind from one end of the world to the other.'

'No, my mum's not called Iris that's for sure, and she can't move round the house that fast,' joked Coroebus as he rummaged in his bag for some bread. Tearing off a chunk he handed some to Demetrios who gratefully took the offering and munched contentedly.

'You know this bread is delicious,' he said between mouthfuls.

'Well it is my part-time job after all; baker and cook. My parents have already got me a job as soon as I leave school, they want me to become the best baker in Greece!'

The pair were laughing and joking so much as they headed off down a small track surrounded by trees that they failed to hear some rustling behind them. Two men, armed with nothing more than a large cloth sack, leapt out of the bushes and ambushed the two friends. Demetrios and Coroebus were bundled unceremoniously into the sack, which was then tied to stop their occupants from escaping.

'Helios never said there was going to be two of them. Lucky it's big enough to hold them both,' Isandros said to his partner in crime.

Lycus shook his head, 'Helios doesn't always give us the right information now does he,' he panted as they toiled with the bulky sack, dragging it back behind the trees and a small rocky outcrop to a waiting horse and cart. The horse was tied to a tree and stood impatiently, and began to whinny when the sack was thrown roughly onto the back of the cart.

Muffled voices could be heard from within, so to lessen the risk of them being discovered extra sacks of wheat and barley were thrown on top. Satisfied that the voices could no longer be heard Lycus turned to his companion and said 'I suppose we better take the cargo and meet up with Helios as planned.'

Demetrios and Coroebus, hidden from sight in their tied sack, could do nothing as the horse and cart rounded the bend and disappeared from sight.

We've Made it Through...

The magic case materialised from the cloud completely unscathed, however their new surroundings were completely alien, as if they'd entered a strange new world. Seconds ago they had been flying high above villages and hills, and now they appeared to be fast approaching a huge temple sat atop a massive mountain. The only concern for them all was just a minute ago the mountain hadn't even been there!

'We've made it through, are you all OK?' Tash asked.

Fluke patted himself down and confirmed he was fine. Appollonia looked pale but otherwise she confirmed that yes, she was still in one piece.

'So this is going to be a really silly question, and forgive me for asking the obvious, but exactly where are we?' Fluke asked, gazing around at their new surroundings in wonderment, 'and where did that mountain come from?'

'Err, to be honest Fluke, I haven't got the foggiest idea,' Appollonia said quietly.

'Less of the fog jokes please, I think *we've all* seen enough fog to last a lifetime!'

The steering still wasn't responding, but the case began to slow and changed direction of its own accord, banking slightly to correct their heading. They were being summoned, it seemed, towards the grand stone temple and Tash was powerless to halt their advance. The case slowed to a complete stop and landed safely on the stone floor. They climbed down and stood staring, unsure what to do next but grateful to at least be on solid ground.

The wispy fog was beginning to disperse, and out of the haze Tash noticed twelve figures sat on huge stone thrones lined up before them.

'Welcome to Mount Olympus,' the ghostly figure sat in the centre spoke, his voice loud and commanded respect. 'You three are the chosen ones...' he looked to his left and right, his eleven colleagues nodded in confirmation, and then he continued, 'I just wish we could have met under different circumstances'.

Fluke stood behind Tash and shoved her gently in the back, propelling her towards the line of stone thrones, and whispered nervously, 'You steered us here, so you can ask who they are and what they want!'

'Please don't be afraid. Step closer so we can have a closer look at you,' another figure commanded gently, a female voice this time.

All three shuffled closer and approached the front. They felt like they were in the presence of greatness and began to bow until the soft voice stopped them.

'Fluke and Tash I believe?' she indicating with her hand, 'and of course the lovely Appollonia. You are all most welcome to our humble home. You, young lady, are the main reason we have summoned you three,' the voice trailed off as she stepped down from her throne and glided over.

'It's my brother isn't it?' Appollonia stepped forward, 'I had this terrible feeling, call it a premonition, that trouble was about to happen, but I never realised it concerned my family...' her voice trailed off as she began to sob.

Fluke and Tash stepped forward. Fluke put a reassuring paw around Appollonia's shoulder to comfort her.

'Who are you all and where are we?' Tash asked, puzzled.

'Search your feelings. You know where you are Tash...' the original voice said. 'And you know who we are and why you're here.'

Mount Olympus –
Home of the Gods...

'Of course, Mount Olympus, home of the Gods...' her voice trailed off, 'you've summoned us here, that's now obvious, but why?'

Fluke spoke up, 'It's our destiny Tash, we've been brought here to help in some way I can feel it. You're the twelve gods of Olympia aren't you? And you must be Zeus?'

'Correct Fluke, you're instinct serves you well,' Zeus confirmed.

'Chosen one's for what?' Appollonia had stopped her crying, and asked the assembled Gods.

'A plan to thwart the smooth running of the newly formed Olympic Games, the Games which incidentally have been introduced in my honour...' Zeus almost looked embarrassed '... will soon take place. An act of evil which unfortunately we cannot directly stop from happening.'

Fluke looked Zeus up and down and noticed he looked coy, *could a God really get embarrassed*, but swiftly discarded the thought as a silly idea.

'But you're all Gods...' Appollonia voiced what Fluke was thinking, 'you can do anything you like, and how does this affect my brother?'

'Your brother is destined for greatness. We cannot allow what *they* have planned to happen without some, how shall we say, assistance from us all,' he turned to the rest for confirmation. 'We as Gods have agreed not to interfere quite so much in what you mortals do anymore.'

A few seconds of silence followed before Tash asked the obvious question, 'So why have we been summoned then? I mean, if you won't get involved, why are we here?'

'He finds it hard to relinquish complete control I'm afraid,' said Hera, Queen of the Gods and sister of Zeus. 'Besides, the games are being held in his honour and we cannot allow any cheating. Any sport, and especially the Olympic Games, should be carried out in the spirit of fairness. Cheats must not be allowed to prosper, the best athlete should always win fairly.'

'But I still don't understand what's going to happen, and who are *they* that you mentioned earlier and why are we here?' said a confused Appollonia.

'A plan has been hatched to kidnap your brother and prevent him from competing in the Games. He's one of the favourites to win the *diaulos* foot race.'

'Really? My brother a favourite? I always beat him.' Appollonia looked surprised.

'That's our Appollonia, nice to see she's back with us!' chuckled Tash.

'Yes, but he'll be taken far away and held prisoner until after the Games, and unfortunately he may be in great danger, as we cannot always see what the future holds.'

'So how do you know all this?' Tash queried.

'Dooh! They're Gods Tash, they just know these things!' said Fluke shaking his head.

'Well, thanks for the compliments, and yes we do know most things but it's actually my brother Hades that told us.'

'Hades? God of the Underworld?' Appollonia voiced her concerns. 'Isn't he the nasty and scary God? I mean people always talk about Hades as a baddie.'

'Ohh, he's not so nasty, he just gets a bad reputation because he lives underground,' laughed Zeus, 'if he was that bad he wouldn't have told us would he? It appears that a kidnap plot has been arranged, the ring leader is pretending to be a messenger from Hades, and he's using my brother's name to scare people into agreeing to carry out his devious tasks.'

'So what have we got to do?' asked Fluke.

'Dooh!' Tash got her revenge and mimicked Fluke. 'It's obvious, Fluke, we've got to rescue

Appollonia's brother,' she said. She paused for a few seconds then said, 'Well I think we have?' she asked hesitantly, afraid she had misunderstood their mission.

'Yes, you must mount a rescue bid, find Demetrios and bring him back in time to compete in the Games.'

The twelve Gods then looked at each other. Deep discussions were taking place when both Apollo and Poseidon, who up until then had kept quite spoke up. 'We don't expect you to carry out this formidable mission on your own. It is filled with danger so we've decided we'll provide you with some assistance, a *little help* to aid you,' they all chuckled, 'and believe us, you'll need all the help you can.'

Looking at each other Fluke and Tash both shrugged their shoulders and turned to Appollonia to see if she knew more, when out of nowhere a huge silent shadow loomed over them, blocking any sunlight. All three looked up to see what had caused the darkness and gasped together as they met the *little help* for the first time.

He Should be Home by Now...

'The house is quiet, Philomela, where is everybody?' Herakleitos asked as he entered the kitchen area. His wife was wringing her hands together nervously.

Turning to face Herakleitos, she said 'Appollonia went off with Fluke and Tash earlier this morning and they haven't returned yet, and Demetrios should be home by now, school finished ages ago. Oh Herakleitos, I'm scared something has happened. How can we lose both son and daughter in the same day?'

'I'm sure they're fine. Fluke and Tash will take good care of Appollonia and Demetrios is bound to have stopped over to see Xene on his way home.'

The conversation was interrupted by a gentle knock at the door. Philomela rushed over, a broad smile etched on her face. 'The silly boy, that must be Demetrios, funny how he knocks though, anybody would think he'd come straight into his own house,' and she threw open the door eagerly, ready to embrace her son.

It wasn't Demetrios. A young girl stood at the threshold with a sorrowful look on her face.

'Xene, my dear, it's lovely to see you again, but where's Demetrios?' Philomela looked over the girl's shoulder, fully expecting to see her son loitering in the background, but Xcnc was alone. 'Haven't you brought him with you?'

'I haven't seen Demetrios for days, as you probably know my dad has barred me from seeing him, but I desperately need to speak to him. I need to make sure he's OK,' said Xene.

Herakleitos approached the open door and said, 'Why wouldn't he be OK? Has something happened that we should know about?'

Xene looked up, 'Look, my dad will go mad if he knows I'm even talking to you, but I overheard him whispering about a kidnap plot...'

'Kidnap plot?' exclaimed Philomela, interrupting Xene.

'Let the girl finish,' said Herakleitos sternly. 'Now carry on, what's this about a kidnapping?'

'It's to do with these new Olympic Games – Dad wants my brother Penthylos to win so badly, and he knows that Demetrios is the clear favourite. He doesn't want to win for my brother's sake or even our village as a whole, but more for himself. He can then swan around claiming he's the leader of a champion village. You know yourself the prestige the winning villages will get from being crowned champions.'

'But kidnapping? I never speak ill of anybody, but even your dad wouldn't stoop that low to kidnap somebody just to win a race.'

'He's changed sir, ever since he's met up with this mystical figure they call the *Hood*. I'm ashamed to admit he's a different person these days.'

The Little Help...

The conversation was brought to a sudden and unexpected end when Philomela caught sight of something flying past the still open door.

'They're back...' she cried out joyfully. 'Well at least we've only lost one of our kids instead of both,' and rushed out the door, closely followed by Xene and Herakleitos.

'Who's back?' asked Xene, slightly confused.

'Appollonia, Fluke and Tash,' Herakleitos said.

'Who's Fluke and Tash?' she replied.

'It's a long story, but for now let's just say they're some new friends of Appollonia and Demetrios.'

They stopped expectantly just outside the front door. A cloud of dust filled the air where the magic case had landed. The dust began to settle and Philomela counted four bodies sat on the case, not the original three that had left earlier this morning.

Fluke and Tash climbed off the case closely followed by Appollonia who came running over to her parents clearly distraught.

'They've got him. Demetrios has been kidnapped,' she cried as she flung herself into her mother's outstretched arms.

'We know...' said Herakleitos, 'Xene has just told us what's happened,' and he glanced back to the magic case and watched as a huge figure stepped down and stood watching the family reunion taking place.

Fluke and Tash were stood side by side with the stranger who dwarfed the pair completely. Whoever he was, he was by far the biggest man that Herakleitos had ever seen before.

'And you are?' asked Herakleitos warily as he strode over.

Tash gently prodded their *little help* in the back, who began to speak.

Heracles...

The giant of a man wearing a lion skin and carrying a huge club strode forward, hand outstretched in a warm and friendly greeting.

'My name is Heracles, son of Zeus. I am here to help find your son.'

Herakleitos, clearly confused with how the day was progressing, shook hands warily with the giant and said 'We are very grateful for your assistance sir, but why would a God and son of Zeus help a normal farming family search for their missing son? What have we done to deserve your help?'

'Apparently Zeus thinks Demetrios is one of the favourites for the Olympic Games, can you believe that?' Appollonia said as she walked over and stood beside her father. 'Ooh, and Heracles here has been asked to help us find him and bring him back in time to compete in the Olympics.'

'Whoa! Slow down my girl, were all still very confused here,' Herakleitos said turning to his wife who looked equally perplexed.

Philomela spoke softly, 'This morning you went off sightseeing and this afternoon you return with

Heracles, the son of Zeus. That's not an everyday occurrence Appollonia, so we'd just like to know what happened in the middle part?' she asked carefully.

Fluke entered the conversation, 'It turns out I'm not the only one who has problems steering our magic case. Tash steered the case right into a big purple cloud and when we flew out the other side we were at Mount Olympus talking to twelve Gods, which trust me is not an everyday occurrence for us either!'

'Summoned to Mount Olympus...' confirmed Tash, 'we were summoned. I didn't really have a say in where we went'.

'Come on, we can discuss this inside,' Philomela ushered everybody indoors just in case any of their neighbours were watching.

'So, you're a real person then?' Herakleitos asked Heracles. 'The myths are true, a real-life God in our house.'

'A demi-god to be precise,' smiled Heracles.

'What's a demi-god?' asked Fluke.

'Half and half. My mother Alcmene was mortal, and my father Zeus, as you know, is a god so therefore immortal.'

'So what Xene say's is true? Her father has arranged to kidnap our son and stop him competing in the games?'

'That just about sums it up...' confirmed Tash. 'And were going to join Heracles and get Demetrios back safely and on time for the start of the competition.'

'We'll get him back, Dad,' Appollonia had a determined look etched on her pretty face.

'What's this *we* business Appollonia? I can't allow you to go, you'll stay here with your mother and I'll find my son,' Herakleitos said.

'No sir...' Heracles stepped forward, 'it has to be your daughter. The Gods of Mount Olympus requested Appollonia, along with Fluke and Tash, all three were summoned. Appollonia is like Demetrios in so many ways, strong-willed, courageous and more than anything else her brother's twin. This could help in the search, she'll have a twin's sixth sense which could be crucial. I'll look after all three of them, that I can promise you.'

Leaving a Trail...

It was hot, dark and very uncomfortable inside the large sack. The horse and cart trundled over rough terrain, every jolt was felt by the pair of friends and Demetrios winced as the cart hit yet another rock.

'Why us?' Demetrios whispered, turning around as best he could to face Coroebus.

Having spent the last hour or so trying unsuccessfully to escape from the sack the best the pair had managed was to tear a small hole which allowed some daylight to filter through.

'I don't know...' Coroebus replied hoarsely. Both of their voices sounded croaky, their initial shouts for help had gone unanswered so they had given up trying, hoping to save some energy. It appeared that nobody was around to hear them anyway, except their kidnappers, and they only laughed. 'I really don't understand what's happening. One minute were walking home from school and the next we've been kidnapped. Did you even see who it was that jumped us?'

'Didn't see a thing, one minute I'm eating your bread and the next someone turned the lights out and it went dark!'

'Bread! Of course...' Coroebus tore off small chunks from his loaf and started to feed it through the small opening they had made.

'What are you doing?' asked Demetrios.

'Leaving a trail...' Coroebus smiled. 'You never know, my baking skills may come in handy after all.'

Back to School...

Herakleitos gave up arguing, it was obvious that Appollonia was going to search for her brother, but the huge question that remained unanswered was where to start.

'At the beginning?' suggested Tash.

'Beginning of what?' asked Fluke.

'Back to school would be as good a place as anywhere. I mean that was the last place we think Demetrios was probably seen.'

It was agreed, they would head over to Demetrios's school, ask a few questions if anybody was still around and see what they could discover.

Philomela, Herakleitos and Xene stood in the doorway and waved off the rescue party headed by Heracles, the magic case strapped firmly to his broad back, closely followed by Fluke, Tash and Appollonia.

'Can you make sense of what's happening...?' Philomela turned to her husband when the rescue party disappeared from sight, 'because this just has to be a bad dream and we're all going to wake up in a minute and everything will be back to normal'.

Herakleitos shook his head, shrugged his shoulders and turned to Xene. 'Where do you think your father would have taken our son? Please Xene, think hard.'

Xene started to sob, tears rolled down her cheeks and she muttered 'I'm so sorry and ashamed that my father would stoop so low and bring this on your family. I don't know where he would take Demetrios, but I will try my best to find out.'

Philomela and Herakleitos both moved over to comfort Xene.

'Stop you're crying, dear,' Philomela whispered, 'We both know how much you love Demetrios, and you can't be blamed for your father's actions.'

Xene stopped her crying and looked up at the two concerned faces. 'I promise you I will try to find out as much as I can. People in our village talk around me as if I'm not there, they don't think I hear them, I mean I'm only a child after all. My father's two friends can't keep a secret, so I will listen in and see what I can find out and report back.'

'Be careful Xene, we can't have you getting into trouble as well as our son,' Herakleitos said.

Xene smiled, 'Oh I'll be careful, I want to find Demetrios safe and well and cheer him on in the Olympic Games!' and hurried out of the door, heading back to her village.

Breadcrumbs...

The rescue party had walked the winding tracks slowly that took them to the small village that housed the local school, taking their time and scanning the ground for any clues. Fluke was the first to approach the front of the small school building. He had taken the lead as they rounded the corner.

'Looks deserted...' he sighed. 'I hoped somebody would be here, looks like we've drawn a blank. We've followed the path in reverse that Demetrios would have taken to walk back home and nothing. No signs and no clues either.'

'What now...?' asked Tash, looking towards Appollonia for any suggestions, 'what if Demetrios went home a different way? Where else could your brother go on his way home?'

Heracles was looking around. Different paths lead off in various directions and he wandered over to join Fluke who was on all fours looking at the dusty ground and carefully studying some bushes.

'Found anything Fluke?' Heracles asked.

'I'm not sure, but I found these footprints in the dust heading down this path, it might be worth looking down here to see if we can find any other clues.'

The four of them regrouped and walked in single file down the dusty track, with Fluke leading the way.

Several minutes of near silence passed as they headed further away from the school.

'Looks like a scuffle took place here,' Heracles knelt down and studied the ground. 'This is where the footprints stop and something heavy was dragged through the dust heading back behind these rocks.' He indicated the marks on the floor. 'This would be a great place for an ambush.'

Appollonia agreed with Heracles and they changed direction and headed behind the rocky outcrop.

'There, over there!' Tash exclaimed excitedly and pointed at two faint lines in the dust, barely visible, but heading off down a long track. 'These looks like marks left by a wheel, maybe a cart of some sort, what do you think?'

'Where does this path lead Appollonia?' Fluke asked.

'I'm not too sure…' she answered, racking her brains, knowing her sixth sense was beginning to take over, 'but I'm sure we're on the right trail, don't ask me how I know, I just do,' and they started following the wheel marks, which eventually disappeared as the track became firmer and the dust was replaced by green grass.

Fluke's keen sense of smell was greater when he was hungry, and his nose was twitching madly. He could smell food but couldn't locate the source.

The party of four carried on walking for a while, desperate to locate some more evidence to confirm that they were still heading in the right direction. Tash was bringing up the rear when the line in front began to slow as they all started to bunch up.

'What's happening up front...' she asked, '... why are we slowing down?'

Heracles was following Fluke and turned around to reply, 'Fluke keeps stopping and eating something, moving on a few steps and then stopping to eat something again. He must be hungry because whatever he's eating he seems to be enjoying it!'

'Food again?' Tash muttered and moved to the front of the line to see what was happening, stood staring down at Fluke who was sniffing the ground eating a trail of white crumbs.

Appollonia joined Tash, stared at the floor, bent down to retrieve some of the crumbs, sniffed them and popped them in her mouth. 'Coroebus! Of course...' she shouted with glee. 'It makes sense now, I would recognise the taste anywhere.'

'What's Coroebus?' asked Fluke standing up, wondering what he'd been eating.

'Not what, but who...' Appollonia's face brightened. 'He's Demetrios best friend and just happens to be a baker, the finest bread maker in Greece. These are breadcrumbs everybody, Fluke's been eating a trail of breadcrumbs that must have been carefully laid by Coroebus. He must have been walking with my brother when the kidnap took place. Well done Fluke, if you weren't always hungry we might have missed the trail!'

With a smile and a new spring in their step, the rescuers headed off down the path following the trail of breadcrumbs, desperate to make up ground on the kidnappers.

Heracles looked at the darkening sky, turned to his three companions and said 'We better think about making a camp for the night, it gets dark quickly once the sun begins to set.'

Tash yawned, which started everybody else yawning as well, 'yes it's been a long day and I could easily curl up and have a nap for a few minutes, how about in here?' she indicated a cave.

The Scary Cave...

Fluke looked inside the cave entrance. 'It looks a bit dark and scary inside, how about we find somewhere else?'

'We'll get a fire going, that will make it nice and cosy and it will keep us warm at night,' said Heracles.

Looking inside Tash said 'and the fire should also keep away any unwanted night-time creatures as well.'

'What night-time creatures?' asked Fluke nervously, now wishing Tash hadn't suggested this particular cave, his eyes trying to adjust to the dark interior, all the time fully expecting to see a whole load of horrible creatures waiting for them.

'Remember what Papa Nummer said?' she said mischievously. 'He told us to be careful of the mythical creatures.'

Fluke laughed nervously. 'Yes, but that was just a joke right? He was winding us up about those creatures, they are just myths aren't they? Heracles, tell Tash there's no such thing as these creatures....' Fluke turned to speak to Heracles, but he had disappeared. 'Where's he gone?' he asked nervously.

'Gone to get some wood to build a campfire and forage for some food, he'll be back in a few minutes,' said Appollonia, 'and yes these mythical creatures do exist Fluke, but we should be OK with Heracles guarding us,' and headed deeper into the cave, closely followed by a sniggering Tash.

'Come on Fluke, keep up. You don't want to stay outside on your own with all those night time creatures lurking behind the bushes!' and burst out laughing.

'It's not funny Tash,' grumbled Fluke hurrying to keep up, warily glancing at the bushes, now convinced that every bush had a creature hidden inside waiting to trap any lonesome walkers.

Appollonia giggled as well. 'Oh leave him alone Tash. Fluke you'll be all right when we get the campfire going.'

Fluke had a confused look on his face as he looked over to Heracles entering the cave. He whispered to Tash, 'I always thought he was called Hercules, so where did Heracles come from?'

'It's an easy mistake to make Fluke. The Romans changed his name for some reason, the spelling is close, but in ancient Greece he's called Heracles.'

They eventually settled down to a night's rest, building their campfire close to the entrance. Food was plentiful as Heracles was a good hunter, used to spending many a night on his own. The flames from the fire cast dancing shadows on the cave walls but failed to penetrate the darkness at the rear of the cave, which just seemed to go on for ever. The thought of what lay deeper in the cave caused Fluke to shiver even though it was warm sat around the fire, and he had a restless night's sleep, trying to keep one eye open for intruders and constantly thinking about what lay deeper in the dark recess of the cave. He eventually fell asleep, joining Tash in a snoring competition, which Heracles and Appollonia both agreed that Tash was winning easily, until eventually they too fell asleep.

The Labyrinth...

Tash woke with a start. Something, a noise maybe, the sound of light footsteps possibly, had woken her from her deep slumber. Glancing around the cave she noticed that last night's fire had all but gone out, just a few burning embers remained. Dawn was fast approaching, the early morning sunshine was winning the battle with the night time as daylight pushed the darkness towards the rear of the cave. She counted two figures huddled up asleep but knew there should be three. She leapt up and hurriedly woke her friends and was faced with the bleary eyed Appollonia and Heracles, both rubbing their eyes and yawning.

'Fluke's missing,' Tash said with panic in her voice.

'Maybe he's gone to fetch some more wood for the fire,' Appollonia said noticing that the fire was nearly out.

'I don't think so Appollonia, he was really nervous last night about all those mythical creatures we were told about before we came here.

He wouldn't go outside on his own, especially as I was winding him up so much.'

Heracles stood, stretched and said, 'Well, we better go and find him before he gets himself into any trouble.' He collected their belongings and strapped the case to his back.

Tash gazed down and noticed paw prints in the dusty floor heading back into the cave. 'Looks like he went that way,' she pointed to the floor, 'but why would he go deeper into the cave?'

Tash led the way, heading back into the darkness, all the time following the trail of paw prints. Heracles took his large club, wrapped some cloth around the end to make a basic lantern, and lit the end from the remains of their fire.

The tunnel they were following split into two paths but thanks to Heracles, the light from his flaming torch enabled them to make out what they hoped was the actual trail left by Fluke. The tunnel they headed down yet again split into two, and they carefully followed the left hand path. Several minutes and many split paths later Tash was worried.

'This is becoming a bit of a maze...' Appollonia said, 'I just hope we can find our way out again,' confirming Tash's worst fears that they could get lost in these tunnels.

'It's called a Labyrinth,' Heracles confirmed, 'and I've got a bad feeling as to what may be at the centre.'

Tash looked at her towering colleague, noticing the change, his face had a concerned look about it. 'Labyrinth?' she whispered, 'isn't that the home of the Mino...' her voice trailed off before she could complete the sentence, as up ahead they spotted Fluke, paws outstretched and walking as if in a daze, heading straight into the centre of a large open space.

'Fluke,' they all whispered urgently, trying to get his attention.

'What's he doing,' asked a confused Appollonia, 'and why doesn't he answer us?'

They caught up with Fluke. Tash stood in front of him waving her paws in front of his face, but he just kept walking straight past her. His eyes were wide open, but he didn't seem to notice she was there.

'He's sleepwalking again!' said Tash. 'He does this occasionally, although this time he could be walking into a trap.'

'Sleepwalking? Why can't we wake him up?' said Appollonia.

'It's best to let them wake up gradually,' confirmed Tash. 'We don't want to startle him, but we can lead him back the way we came,' and she took hold of an outstretched paw and carefully turned him around.

The Minotaur...

Tash, holding Flukes paw, gazed around at their surroundings and was immediately confused. She spied several entrances around the cave walls, each one looked exactly the same as the next and she couldn't remember which one they had used, and it was now clear they were at the centre of the Labyrinth.

A deep bellowing sound came from one of the tunnel entrances. The frightening noise rolled down the tunnel and seemed to shake the stone walls.

'What was that, and why are you holding my paw?' asked Fluke, now fully awake.

'Oh welcome back, so now you decide to wake up,' said Tash, releasing Fluke's paw she explained, 'You've been sleepwalking again and led us down here.'

'Down where?' asked Fluke, gazing around the cave.

'To the centre of the Labyrinth, Fluke.'

'So you mean the cave we slept in last night was the entrance to the Labyrinth, the home of the Minotaur...?' he shivered at the thought. 'So these mythical creatures do exist after all!' and jumped as another scary bellowing noise came from one the tunnels. This time the noise was really loud and seemed to be getting closer.

'We've got to get out of here, and quick!' Appollonia confirmed what everybody was thinking.

'Too late...' said Heracles looking over at one of the entrances, 'you'd better stand back and let me deal with this,' as a creature that looked even larger and stronger than Heracles entered the Labyrinth.

Tash looked over and studied the huge beast. The creature that stood over seven feet tall on two legs was part bull and part man. The large head of a bull with a stunning pair of sharp horns, with the body and powerful-looking legs of a man. Its long tail swished angrily as it stared at its new victims. The creature gazed over at the four figures stood side by side and bellowed again, the sound rolled around the chamber and plumes of moisture streamed from its flared nostrils.

The quick-thinking Tash asked Heracles for their magic case. He slid it off his back and laid it on the floor.

'What are you doing Tash?' asked Fluke, his eye's glancing between Tash and the Minotaur.

'I've had an idea, Fluke. Remember Nottingham Castle?'

'How could I possibly forget...,' Fluke shivered at the thought, 'but what's that got to do with this creature,' and looked back over at the Minotaur.

'What's Nottingham Castle?' Appollonia asked warily, staring with fascination at the bellowing beast which had started to move towards them.

'No time to explain,' said Tash working fast to open the case. The lid sprung open and she reached inside, rummaged around and pulled out Flukes red cape he last wore what seemed like ages ago. 'Fluke, now's the time to be a hero, you'll have to keep the Minotaur busy while we try to figure a way out of this mess,' and handed Fluke his red cape.

'Oh gee, thanks Tash, just the perfect way to start a new day!' he said, but took hold of the cape and stood to one side near the cave wall. The Minotaur stopped his advance and glared at the red cape.

'Why the cape?' asked a bewildered Heracles.

Fluke the matador...

'I'm hoping that bulls from Greece are the same as the bulls from Spain,' said Tash, and waited to see what the beast was going to do next.

Sure enough, Tash's instincts proved correct. The Minotaur was glaring angrily at the red cape. Fluke played the part and was getting into his new role, shouting and flapping the red cape.

The half bull, half man charged, the new arrivals temporarily forgotten as this new red intruder needed his full attention. Fluke was a bag of nerves but just at the right moment stepped aside and swiped his red cape away. The creature skidded to a stop several feet past Fluke and was confused as to why he hadn't yet caught this red thing.

The Minotaur turned quickly and charged again, '*Olé, Olé,*' Fluke shouted as he stepped to one side and whipped the red cape away for the second time. The beast skidded past and crashed headlong into the stone wall which only angered it even more.

Heracles was watching with interest at the antics of Fluke, whilst Tash shut the case and quickly set the controls to manual on the case.

Fluke was backing away from the beast as with each pass the Minotaur was getting closer. He began inching his way around the exterior wall of the cave and ended up near an entrance. Looking over he saw Tash fiddling with the controls of their case.

'Get ready Fluke, we'll be there in a minute,' she shouted and instructed Heracles and Appollonia to hop on board. Tash followed, sat at the front and patted the case, 'C'mon, time to save Fluke. Heracles, when we pass by, grab Fluke and pull him on board.'

The magic case lifted off the floor, hovered for a second until Tash steered towards the retreating Fluke.

'I might not have a minute,' he shouted back, not having the time to see how Tash was getting on. The beast charged again, getting closer with each pass; the sharp horns tore some of Fluke's clothing as he got close, way too close for Fluke's comfort who backed away, trod on the red cape, stumbled, and fell in a heap on the floor.

The Minotaur sensing victory charged at the now helpless Fluke caught up in his red cape. Just before the Minotaur reached his victim, the case flew past and the super strong arm of

Heracles scooped up a startled Fluke and bundled him onto the back of the case.

'Now let's get out of here…' Appollonia whooped with excitement as the magic case tore through an entrance and down the tunnel, scraping the wall slightly but at least they were heading away from the angry beast.

'Which way?' asked Tash over her shoulder.

'Left up ahead, then right, and two left turns,' said Fluke.

'No, turn right, then right again, and then a left,' Heracles said.

'No…' Appollonia shouted, 'two lefts and then two right turns'.

'Whoa, one at a time please,' Tash shouted back and had to make a split-second choice as she was faced with two tunnels. Taking Fluke's advice she headed down the left tunnel and then took a sharp right turn followed by two left turns. Speeding up and desperate to be out of the maze they flew down the tunnel.

'I can see light at the end of the tunnel,' Tash exclaimed with glee, but her joy was short-lived as they sped through the entrance only to find themselves re-enter the main cave, having entered from the opposite side to the one they had left only a minute ago. Shooting straight past a startled looking Minotaur, the creature, thinking he had lost his prey, fairly grinned as he gave chase. Fluke made the mistake of looking over his shoulder and panic swept through him as the half bull creature was closing rapidly, his sharp horns only inches away from Fluke's back.

'Err, if you could speed up Tash it would be nice!' and he risked another glance behind, 'and if you could pass me your club please Heracles'.

The club was handed over with Fluke swinging blindly. With more luck than anything else, he bopped the Minotaur on its head, causing the charging beast to slow down and shake his head in frustration which gave them a few extra seconds and a good head start in the chase.

The case sped down more tunnels, Tash didn't know where they were going, and all the time the Minotaur was gaining ground, until Tash recognised some markings on the tunnel walls. The magic case tore at some speed down a tunnel, with daylight appearing ahead and this time her choice proved the correct one. They flew past the spot they had slept last night, the fire now completely out, and flew out of the cave entrance into fresh air. Circling around and at a safe height they witnessed the charging bull stop at the entrance to its Labyrinth, clearly angry that his victims had escaped.

'Phew, that was a close one,' muttered Tash, 'and I think when we pick tonight's accommodation we'll be extra careful'.

'I told you to choose another cave...' grinned Fluke, 'but as usual nobody listens to me!' and they all laughed at their narrow escape.

Where's Dad?...

Xene had returned back to her village, desperate to find out any information about Demetrios. Her father, usually wandering around the village or sat around the *agora* talking to the village elders, was nowhere to be seen. Disgruntled, she headed home to see if by some chance he was there. Entering the main door she witnessed her mother carrying out her daily chores, singing quietly and happily to herself. Noticing her daughter enter the room she enquired, 'And where have you been young lady?'

'Why, has dad asked where I am?' Xene was wondering if her dad had mentioned that he had caught her eavesdropping on his conversation.

'Your father? No Xene, but *I* was worried, it's not like you to disappear without letting me know where you're going.'

'I've been to see Demetrios's mum and dad, apparently he's missing, and...'

'Missing? What do you mean missing?' Orithyia interrupted her daughter.

'He's late home from school. Have you heard anything?' Xene asked casually, hopeful her mother may have some information.

'Why would I hear anything? Besides, he's probably off with his best friend Coroebus, those two are always together.

'Where's dad?' Xene asked.

'Your father told me he has some business to attend to, and won't be back until late tomorrow. He was muttering to himself about these new Olympic Games, and mentioned he was heading over the mountains to Tropaia.'

'Tropaia? That's a distance to travel, it must about 25 dolichos away.'

'Yes Xene, that's why he won't be back until tomorrow. Why are you suddenly interested in your father's business? You don't normally take much notice.'

Xene shrugged. 'No reason mother, just wondering,' and shuffled back out of the door, turning her head she shouted to her mum, 'I'll be back soon mum, see you later,' and scurried off before her mother could argue with her.

Heading back out of the village Xene stopped at her father's small stable. She cast her eyes around the open space, finally resting on a grand-looking white stallion. *Strange* she thought to herself, *I don't remember my father ever owning a fine looking stallion such as this*, and hurried over. She leapt up onto the broad white back, whispered soothing words and guided her mount onto the path that would lead her back to see Demetrios's mum and dad. She needed to pass on the information she had just heard from her mother. *Why Tropaia?* She wondered to herself, *what was there that would make her dad travel a day and half round trip?* Maybe Herakleitos or Philomela could make any sense of the situation, but she knew that whatever was in Tropaia must be important and she headed off, her stallion was picking up speed, sensing time was important her new companion flew like the wind leaving Xene breathless.

Zeus leaves a sign...

Zeus was sat on his huge throne looking down into a stone bowl balanced on his knees, currently filled with a magical silvery liquid. This bowl of liquid in the hands of an Olympian god was equivalent to our modern day television. Zeus watched with interest as he saw from the top of Mount Olympus, Xene leaving her mothers and hurrying over to the neighbouring village with the news she had just learnt.

'What are you watching now, my brother?' asked his sister Hera, smiling to herself, 'I thought you weren't going to get too involved?' she laughed, 'but you just can't help yourself, you have to meddle in the human affairs don't you?'

'It's not meddling,' Zeus said looking up from his bowl, 'it's helping the mortals, just a little bit of help is all they need,' and glanced back to his viewing bowl.

'And how is watching them going to help?' Hera asked gently.

'By steering Fluke and Tash in the right direction. I've given them a small sign which I hope they will pick up on, plus a surprise gift to Xene which should come in handy. They've all done well so far, picking up the trail of breadcrumbs, and managing to escape from the Minotaur, it really does make fascinating viewing.'

Hera laughed and stepped down from her throne and almost glided off, ghost-like, to do whatever Greek Gods and Goddesses did during the day, leaving Zeus to wonder what sort of sign he was going to leave the intrepid rescue party.

A Sign From Above...

After their narrow escape from the Labyrinth, Tash landed the magic case at a safe distance and they resumed their pursuit of the kidnappers on foot and paw and, with the case strapped securely to the back of Heracles, they headed off.

'The trail of breadcrumbs has stopped, they must have run out,' Fluke confirmed, sniffing the ground to see if he could locate any more of the tasty morsels.

'Or you've eaten all the bread, Fluke,' Tash giggled.

'We'll have to find another sign,' Heracles said turning to Appollonia.

'That was very clever of your brother to leave us a trail like that,' he confirmed.

'That wouldn't be my brother, he's not smart enough! It must have been Coroebus idea, he's the clever one,' Appollonia joked with her colleagues, 'I think were still heading in the right direction though, it just somehow feels right.'

The morning was warm, and as they walked off Fluke was looking around at the scenery of far-off mountains, and the surrounding trees which stood tall and majestic. Gazing up at the blue sky he commented, 'what a lovely day for a walk in the woods'.

'It will be even better if we could find Demetrios and Coroebus...' said Tash. 'We've got to find a sign, more breadcrumbs or anything to confirm that we've not taken a wrong turn.'

'We'll find something Tash, I just know we will, but until we do, let's enjoy the glorious weather, a nice bit of sunshine and a clear blue sky. Well, almost a clear blue sky, all except that silly little cloud, I'm sure it's been following us for the last hour.'

'Don't be daft, how can a cloud follow us?' Tash laughed and sped up to catch up with Heracles and Appollonia.

Fluke shrugged, took another look at the cloud and thought it had changed shape, it looked a little bit like a hand, *now I'm imagining things* he muttered to himself and caught up with Tash.

They walked for another hour, a solid hike, until Heracles found a ring of stones and suggested they sit and rest for a while, eat some food and discuss their options.

Sat around in a circle, they talked and passed around some drinking water that Heracles had got from a mountain spring.

'Look Tash,' Fluke pointed up to the sky, 'our cloud's still following us and I know it sounds strange but if you look closely it looks like a hand with a finger pointing over to those mountains'.

Tash looked up at Fluke's cloud, and had to agree it did look like a cloudy finger pointing the way. 'This is going to sound silly, but Fluke is right you know, that cloud has been following us. Appollonia, what's over the other side of that mountain?'

She gazed up at the single white cloud, looked at the direction it was pointing and said 'Tropaia. It's a little place called Tropaia, and I have a feeling it's a sign, my instincts are now beginning to suggest we head over there. C'mon everybody, follow that cloud!'

Prison Cell...

A shadowy figure passed by the solid wooden door, paused, and looked through a small crack in the wooden frame. He saw two figures huddled in the far corner asleep. Satisfied that everything was quiet, he walked off.

'He's gone...' one of the curled-up figures whispered to his friend, 'but I'm sure he'll be back soon, he seems to pass by, check up on us, and then come back later to check on us again.'

Coroebus rolled over to face his best friend 'Good...' His whispered reply only reached the ears of his fellow prisoner. 'We can carry on digging.' He leapt up urgently and began frantically digging with a bit of wood they had found in the corner of the room. He worked and talked at the same time. 'Any ideas where we are Demetrios?'

'Not sure...' Demetrios was helping the best he could with another piece of wood, 'but I did notice the air was colder at one point when we were on the back of the cart, so I figure we've crossed the mountains and come down the other side'.

Looking around their large dark room they were being held in, Demetrios was searching for a place to put the soil they had dug up. They had started to dig by the back wall, and hoped to dig under and make their escape. With nowhere obvious to hide the small pile of dirt, they had eventually agreed to pile it up by the far wall beside the door and hope it wouldn't be spotted by their captors who had been spying on them.

'I hear footsteps, quick, cover the hole and pretend to be asleep again.'

Demetrios dragged the cloth sack they had been captured in and covered the hole in the ground, the pair then laid either side of the sack.

They waited a minute then heard the shuffled footsteps retreat away from the door. Turning to face each other they both sighed, took hold of their pieces of wood and began to dig. *It is going to be a long day*, thought Demetrios.

Not Another Cave...

Heracles had taken the lead, closely followed by Appollonia, who had both set a fast pace as they trekked up the side of the steep mountain following the cloud shaped like a hand with a pointing finger.

'It must be Zeus helping us,' chuckled Heracles. 'He likes to play games, and look...' he pointed to the ground 'we've managed to pick up a trail again! Wheel marks in the dirt, so we're definitely on the right track, although there are two sets of wheel marks, so looks like two carriages have passed through here recently' and they carried on following the tracks up the side of the mountain.

Passing a cave entrance, one set of the tracks disappeared inside and the other set carried on. Fluke looked warily into the cave entrance and said, 'Oh not another cave, are you sure this is a good idea stopping here? You know what happened last time we entered a cave.'

'We have to Fluke,' Appollonia said. 'One of these the trails goes inside and if we have a chance of rescuing my brother then I'm going in, regardless of what's waiting for us.'

Fluke followed Appollonia inside, with Heracles and Tash close behind. Following the tracks they entered deeper into the cave, one long tunnel which thankfully didn't have too many twists and turns. The tracks just kept going until eventually they entered a large open space, which, surprisingly, was full of stone statues. They stood together, huddled in the centre of the room wondering who had built these stone figures and why anybody would keep them stored here.

Tash's keen hearing picked up a hissing sound coming from the other side of the dark room. They all then heard the same noise as it got steadily closer.

'That sound, it reminds me of a load of hissing snakes...' Fluke whispered nervously, his voice trailing off as he suddenly remembered some of the stories that Papa Nummer had mentioned back home. 'Quick Heracles, get the magic case open.'

Heracles, sensing the urgency, slipped the case off his back and onto the ground and watched with interest as Fluke reached deep inside. With a triumphant shout, Fluke pulled out two sets of swimming goggles.

Tash looked on with a confused expression on her face and said, 'Swimming goggles, Fluke? Off for a paddle on the way home are we? I didn't think you could swim.'

'Mirrored swimming goggles, Tash, that we used in Ancient Egypt! Remember what Papa Nummer said about Medusa and her head full of live venomous snakes? If you look into the snakes eyes they turn you to stone, well these might give us some protection.'

It suddenly dawned on them all as they looked over at the statues. Every one of the stones was a human figure and they realised with horror that this must be the home of *Medusa*.

'These poor people must have camped here the night and been turned to stone.' Fluke tapped one figure closest to him and his paw felt the cold stone, causing him to shiver.

Snakes and Ladders...

'I hate snakes!' exclaimed Heracles backing off, 'it's my biggest fear!'

Fluke and Tash quickly slipped on their mirrored swimming goggles and told Heracles and Appollonia to turn around, find a safe hiding place and not to look at *Medusa*.

Tash looked around, her gaze rested on an old wooden cart which one of these poor victims must have wheeled in with him. She then looked a few feet up, and pointed. 'Up there on that ledge, you can hide behind some rocks.'

'How are we going to climb up there?' Appollonia said as she saw the ledge that Tash had indicated.

'In that wooden cart...' Tash indicated with her paw '... is what looks like a wooden ladder, prop it up against the wall and climb up as fast as you can.'

Heracles was quick, he rummaged in the cart and dragged out the rickety wooden ladder, and leant it against the wall.

'It doesn't look very safe,' he muttered.

'It has to be safer than looking at her,' Fluke exclaimed and pointed to a female figure that glided out of the darkness, her head was full of hissing snakes. 'Sorry, make that two creatures,' he corrected himself as a second creature slithered alongside.

'They say things come in three's Fluke, look another one!' Tash gasped as a third figure joined the party.

'The Gorgon sisters – Medusa, Stheno and Euryale, so they really do exist,' Fluke muttered, 'Papa Nummer was right, Tash.'

'The Nummers are always right, Fluke, you should know that by now,' and she turned her attention back to the three sisters who stood in front of them.

Fluke noticed out of the corner of his eye that Heracles and Appollonia had scaled the rickety wooden ladder and were hidden behind some rocks high up on the ledge.

'Playing snakes and ladders will never be the same again, Tash,' he joked, referring to the board game they had played several times at home, then became serious as he wondered what their next move would be.

Fluke tapped Tash on the head a couple of times with his paw, causing Tash to yelp 'Ouch! What was that for?' she queried rubbing a paw on her sore head.

'Just checking you've not been turned into stone,' he joked. 'What do we do now, Tash?'

'Well you can stop hitting my head for a start,' she said. 'But you've made a good point, Fluke – so far so good, we've been staring at the Gorgon sisters for a minute now and we've not turned to stone and are still furry!'

'So these darkened mirrored swimming goggles work then?' Fluke puffed his chest out in pride.

Tash put one paw in front of another and with Fluke at her shoulder they both walked a bit closer to close the gap. The hissing noise increased in volume as the snakes got angry. The sisters had a confused look on their faces, *why weren't these two creatures turning to stone?*

One of the sisters, angry that her magic powers seemed useless, strode forward to stare directly into the faces of Fluke and Tash, willing them to turn into stone. As she got closer she caught sight of her own hideous face in the reflection of Fluke's mirrored swimming goggles. She gasped out loud at the sight of her own face, and screamed as her own reflection turned her into stone.

Confused, the two remaining sisters began to back off, obviously afraid that whatever had happened to their sister could easily happen to them as well.

Sensing victory, Tash shouted out *Chaaarge* and ran after the retreating Gorgon sisters who had turned and fled the room.

Returning a few seconds later Tash confirmed, 'they've disappeared down another tunnel, so come on, let's get out of here while the coast is clear,' and watched as Heracles and Appollonia slid down the ladder and joined Fluke and Tash as they beat a hasty retreat back down the opposite tunnel and headed back to freedom.

Once outside, Fluke turned to Tash and said 'I knew these goggles would come in handy again one day,' and whipped off his goggles.

'Err, a hideous looking creature,' Tash joked pointing to Fluke, 'no wonder those two sisters legged it,' and they all fell about laughing, realising again how close they had come to nearly being the Gorgon sisters latest stone ornaments.

Appollonia eventually stopped laughing and said, 'OK, so now we know the other tracks must be the ones we need to keep following, so c'mon let's get moving!' and they headed off, following the wheel marks which headed towards the village of Tropaia.

All Downhill...

The air was getting thinner the higher up the mountain they got, with both Fluke and Tash panting as Appollonia set a brisk pace, desperate to be reunited with her brother.

The trees were thinning out and the landscape was changing from lush green forest to flinty stone and rocks. They reached the summit and gazed back down the way they had walked. The foot of the mountain was a few miles down and the cave where they had encountered Medusa was some way back. Feeling tired but safe in the knowledge they were at least heading in the right direction, they looked over the other side of the mountain and down at the small village of Tropaia nestled neatly at the foot of the mountain.

'Some way to go, but at least it's all downhill from here,' Tash stood breathing deeply the fresh mountain air, paws resting on her hips.

'Yes, and no more caves, please tell me there's no more caves!' exclaimed Fluke, only half joking.

'We'll get our breath back for a few minutes then head off,' Appollonia confirmed, pointing down the valley, and then looked at the sun beginning to set 'and if my brother and Coroebus are there, we'll rescue them at dawn. Most people will either still be snoozing or just waking up, always a good timc to catch people unawares and off-guard.'

Heracles confirmed they would make a hasty descent, get as far down the mountain as they could before night fall, make camp and prepare for the dawn raid in the morning.

Off to Tropaia...

Xene gently pulled on her stallion's mane and slowed down as she was fast approaching the house. The door was flung open and both Philomela and Herakleitos rushed out to greet her, *they must have been waiting by the door for any news on their son* thought Xene sadly.

'Tropaia...' she gasped trying to get her breath back to talk, the ride had been quick, her horse was very fast and the journey from her own village hadn't taken long. 'My dad has gone to talk business over at Tropaia, something to do with the new Olympic Games. I'm going there now to see what more information I can find out.'

'That's a fair ride, Xene,' said Philomela. 'It'll take ages to get there.'

'Not with my trusty new companion. He's fast, the fastest I've ever ridden,' she smiled as she gently patted her stallions head, ruffling it's mane.

'Be careful then my girl, we're dealing with some nasty people here, anybody capable of kidnap should not be treated lightly, you may end up a victim as well,' said Herakleitos, concern etched in his face.

'I'll be extra careful, I promise,' Xene studied the worried faces below, 'I've got to try and team up with Appollonia, Fluke, Tash and Heracles. Together we stand a chance, I have a good feeling, don't ask me how I know, I just know it will all be OK.' Hoping she sounded more confident than she actually felt she steered her stallion away from the house, deep down she was nervous, hoping her brave words would come true.

'Bring our boy back safely Xene, please,' she heard Philomela from behind as she galloped away.

Dawn Raid...

They had made camp on the outskirts of the village, hiding in some bushes for the night. Their journey down the mountain had been a lot quicker than going up had been, although the last couple of miles had been in complete darkness, with Tash and her keen eyesight carefully leading the way.

They had taken it in turns to rest their eyes for an hour or so, with at least one of them staying awake to keep guard and listen out for any trouble.

'Did you manage any sleep?' yawned Fluke, scratching an itchy spot behind his ear.

'Just a short catnap, Fluke, although I'm too nervous to sleep properly,' she confirmed.

They were both startled by the looming figure of Heracles returning quietly to their hidden camp.

'I've just had a quick look around the village whilst it's still dark,' he explained, 'it all seems quiet, except a large farmhouse surrounded by fencing at the far end of the village, it looks like a fortress and they've had a lantern burning inside all night long behind the wooden shutters so someone has been awake all night'.

'We'll try there first,' whispered Appollonia, and made ready to leave the safety of their hideout but was stopped in her tracks when she noticed Tash sniffing the air. 'What is it Tash?' she asked.

'Dogs, Appollonia, I can smell a dog,' Tash said warily, 'and not all dogs are as friendly with cats as Fluke is, we cats have had to learn to be very careful.'

Fluke sniffed the air and confirmed 'Yep, I can smell a dog Tash, but it's strange, doesn't smell like a normal kind of dog...' his voice trailed off as Appollonia rose from the bushes and said, 'Dog or no dog, we're getting my brother back, besides we had a pet dog which I used to take out for a walk every day and he was OK,' and began to creep carefully towards the farmhouse.

'I'll look after you, Tash,' Fluke confirmed, following Appollonia and Heracles. 'I'm not afraid of *any* dog,' he continued a bit more bravely than he actually felt, because inside he was a bag of nerves and hoped the dog they could smell wasn't going to be too big.

They crept around the outside of the village which was still in semi-darkness, dawn was fast approaching and the early morning sun was due up any minute. They all got spooked and jumped as a cockerel from the farmhouse they were approaching sang out his dawn chorus of *cock-a-doodle-doo*. They halted and waited to see if there was any movement, but nothing was stirring inside or outside so they pressed on, Appollonia taking the lead.

Tash's hackles were up which made Fluke titter to himself. 'Well look at you Tash, you look twice as big with your fur all stuck up like that, what's the matter?'

'That doggy smell is getting closer Fluke and something's not right,' she said as they all slowed down, the fence was now the only barrier between themselves and the farmhouse, which was hopefully holding Demetrios and Coroebus.

Looks like Cerberus, Hound of the Underworld...

They climbed over the fence easily, except Fluke who had managed to get his woollen tunic stuck on a splinter of wood and was left hanging upside down.

Tash turned and joked, 'Hanging upside down again, Fluke? If it's not trees it's a fence,' and she watched as Fluke managed to unhook himself and clamber safely over the fence, eventually he caught up with the rest as they entered the courtyard area of the farmhouse.

Moving carefully towards the house the quiet morning was suddenly ended by a very loud growling noise coming from a rickety looking wooden shelter that stood like a guardhouse close to the front door. A large creature which resembled a dog began to emerge from its kennel, although this was plainly not your average family pet, as it had three heads and a serpent like snake for a tail.

'What is it? Smells like a dog, but looks nothing like any dog I've ever seen before' asked a startled Fluke.

'Looks like Cerberus, hound of the underworld,' stated Heracles. 'Zeus's brother Hades has a similar creature but it's not the same dog, although it must be the same breed.'

'So, you're not afraid of *any* dog then Fluke is what I think you said only five minutes ago.' Tash looked over at her companion and continued, 'And correct me if I'm wrong Fluke, but I'm pretty sure you said you'll look after me as well,' and gave Fluke a nervous smile and playfully shoved him in the back propelling him closer to the creature.

'Walkies! C'mon boy, fancy a walk?' Fluke patted his leg whilst whispering to the three-headed dog and turned to his colleagues. 'So Appollonia, do you fancy taking *that* dog for a walk then?' Fluke joked nervously, looking at the beast that stood guarding the house.

'How are we going to get past him to get inside?' Appollonia said, but was suddenly distracted by movement from the side of the property.

Something was being thrown away from the side of the house. Appollonia and Heracles quietly walked over and stood watching as they witnessed soil being thrown, someone inside was trying to dig under the wall. Stepping closer she glanced down at the floor and watched as two pairs of hands inside the building were trying to make the hole bigger.

'Demetrios?' she asked quickly, 'is that really you?'

Both pairs of hands stopped their digging and a muffled voice from within said, 'Appollonia? What are you doing here? Quick help us get the hole bigger.' She fell to her knees with joy and started digging with her hands. Heracles knelt beside her, his massive hands quickly helped make a bigger hole. Reaching inside he dragged Demetrios and then helped Coroebus scramble free from their prison.

Demetrios stood blinking and wiped soil away from his face. 'Well you took your time,' he smiled as his sister gave him a big hug and then she playfully punched him on the arm.

'What was that for?' he grinned.

'For leaving me to train on my own! Don't you ever leave me again,' she joked, and then a serious note entered her voice. 'We have to get out of here before we wake the whole house.'

'Who's with you?' Demetrios looked up at the towering Heracles, and then remembered his manners. 'But whoever you are thank you for helping my sister. Is it just the two of you?'

'It's a long story and I'll explain after we've got you home safely. Fluke and Tash are here somewhere...' her voice trailed away as she glanced over and saw the three-headed dog was loose and had begun padding over towards Fluke.

Who's a Good Boy Then...?

Tash gulped nervously as the three-headed creature began to make its way over. It stopped its growling and tilted its head to one side as if studying the two trespassers.

'What now?' Tash asked Fluke. 'The fence is back that way, do you think you can make it before it starts to chase us?'

'I'm hoping it won't chase us, Tash,' said Fluke as he rummaged inside his tunic, found what he was looking for and began to walk carefully over to the guard dog. He reached out and let the dog sniff whatever Fluke had in his paw.

Appollonia and the rest joined Tash and watched as Fluke stopped in front of the three headed hound and began whispering. Astounded, they watched in disbelief as Fluke fed the beast a dog biscuit and then began to pat the dog and ruffle his three furry heads.

'Who's a good boy then?' Fluke said making a fuss of the dog. 'He's OK everybody, he just needs a stroke and some dog biscuits, come and see,' and moved aside as the guard dog rolled over on its back and let everybody join in the stroking and petting.

'Some guard dog that is,' boomed a familiar angry voice from the door. 'I always said that dog was too soft.'

They stopped their fussing of the dog and looked up. Nobody had noticed the front door had been opened and Demetrios and Appollonia looked towards the figures they both instantly recognised. Standing on the front porch was Helios with his two colleagues, Isandros and Lycus, and at least twenty of the *Hood's* own men, completely outnumbering the rescue party.

Flying Horse to the Rescue...

A shadow flew over the two groups facing each other, neither noticed, and the kidnappers ended the tense standoff and began marching towards the small group.

'Why Helios? Why kidnap my brother? Is it because you don't approve of my brother dating your daughter?' asked Appollonia angrily.

Helios laughed and gave an evil chuckle. 'To win a huge bet, it's as simple as that. I stand to inherit acres of farmland if your brother loses the *diaulos* foot race. The *Hood* has bet with all the other villages that my son Penthylos will win the race, but we all know he stands no chance against your brother, so it was easier to make sure Demetrios didn't get the chance to compete. The *Hood* is paying me in farmland which is worth a fortune to make sure your brother doesn't win, so as you can see there is a lot at stake. It was an added bonus that his friend Coroebus was with him during the kidnapping, it means I stand to win double the amount of land now as Penthylos can win both *diaulos* foot race and the *stadion* race.'

Out of nowhere another familiar voice shouted, 'Dad, how could you betray our friends, and all for a piece of land.'

They all looked up and gasped as a white stallion flew overhead, circled once and landed on the ground separating the kidnappers and rescue party.

'Xene!' shouted Demetrios gleefully and rushed over to embrace his girlfriend.

'Pegasus?' queried Heracles with a grin and walked over to stroke the huge white stallion 'Where did you two come from?'

'I found him in dad's stable and rode as fast as possible to help you, we literally flew like the wind,' Xene gasped getting her breath back, ruffling Pegasus's mane of hair.

'I think my dad Zeus has been helping again,' Heracles muttered to himself, a smile spread from ear to ear as he continued patting Pegasus.

Xene turned towards her father, who for once was nearly speechless at the sight of his normally quiet and timid daughter riding on a flying horse.

'Dad, you have to let them go, what you've done is wrong.'

Helios replied, 'I'm afraid it's too late, Xene. The Olympic Games start this afternoon and you need to register your names before you enter. Oh, and in case you hadn't noticed, you're a very long way from home so you and your friends will never make it back in time,' and with a smug look he turned to his colleagues and instructed them to recapture Demetrios and Coroebus and hold them until after the games had started.

We'll Call You Bark-at-us...

As Helios and the *Hood's* men approached Demetrios, they heard a low growl which rose in volume. Fluke and Tash turned around and saw their new friend get to his paws and push past Heracles to stand facing his former masters. The three-headed dog first looked at Helios, and then over to Fluke, Tash and the rest. It had a choice to make. Back to being chained up in a kennel, fed small scraps of food, never get walked and petted *or* he could be fed dog biscuits, stroked, tickled and probably walked. It was an easy choice.

The loudest bark anybody had ever heard came at once from all three of the heads, scaring Helios and his gang so much they turned around and fled back towards the safety of the house, slamming the door behind them.

'I thought you said that dog of yours was soft,' questioned a breathless Isandros, still visibly shaken from their encounter and peering through the window as the dog returned to its new owners.

Tash looked at the early morning rising sun.

She turned to Demetrios and Coroebus and said, 'We better get a move on if we're going to get back in time to register you two for the Games.'

Fluke meanwhile was getting to know their new friend. 'I think we better give our new companion a name Tash, what do you suggest?'

The hound sat in front of the group, tail wagging in joy and feasting on dog biscuits that Fluke had kindly been feeding him, whilst everybody made a fuss of their new friend. The three heads started barking again, and Appollonia turned and asked 'Why does he still bark at us?'

'I've run out of biscuits,' said Fluke noting that three heads took a lot more feeding than the normal one, 'but I think you've found the ideal name for our new friend, we'll call him *Bark-at-us*, that sounds like a great Greek name.' They all laughed and agreed the name was perfect.

Xene, Demetrios, Coroebus and Heracles climbed on the back of Pegasus, and made ready to fly back home.

Tash, Appollonia and Fluke climbed on their magic case and they looked over at Bark-at-us. 'We're going to take him with us aren't we Tash?' Fluke asked, 'I mean we can't leave him behind with that lot,' he said pointing to the faces peering through the window.

'Of course he's coming with us, Fluke. C'mon boy hop aboard.'

Bark-at-us didn't need to be asked twice and he leapt up behind Fluke. He rested one of his three heads on one shoulder, another head on the other shoulder and the third head rested on top of Flukes head.

'Lead the way Pegasus!' they all shouted as the majestic white stallion took to the air and flew off towards home. Tash turned the handle on the magic case three times, the case hovered above the ground and turned to follow Pegasus.

Helios looked on in dismay. His dreams of becoming a wealthy landowner were disappearing as quickly as Pegasus and the magic case as they flew up and over the mountain and disappeared from sight, his only hope now was if they failed to register their names in time for the Olympic Games.

Registration...

Aristos and Keos stood scratching their heads wondering exactly how many people were queued up to register their names to enter as competitors for the very first Olympic Games. Both men had volunteered to help with the registration process and both figured it would be an easy day, little did they realise this new event would have proved so popular and brought so many people along. They stood gazing down the long line of applicants, all of whom were eagerly waiting patiently in line to sign their names up.

Along with the dozens of applicants, there were many thousands of spectators that lined the stadium, all cheering wildly, eager to see friends and family represent their local villages, and keen for the games to start. There was nothing a Greek liked better than a good sporting event.

'We should be finished in an hour or so,' Keos said to Aristos carefully scribing another name down on some papyrus parchment along with the event the athlete had chosen to enter, 'I mean we've already got loads of names down on the list for most of the events taking place'.

Aristos was also scribing the same names as a duplicate copy, but instead of papyrus parchment he was using a wet clay tablet, writing with a reed pen made from a cut and shaped single reed straw or a small length of bamboo. This wet clay tablet was then left out in the sun to dry and would then be collected along with the papyrus and stored away as a backup record of who had entered which event.

'Do you think they'll hold the event again?' Aristos said to his colleague, busily writing a new name and event down on his tablet.

'I guess so,' said Keos, 'I've heard a rumour that the organisers are planning to hold these events every Olympiad, and I guess looking at the number of spectators it's already proving popular.'

Keos was interrupted by a huge gasp coming from the crowds in the stands. Looking over he noticed they were all gazing up to the sky. Shielding the sun from his eye's he followed their gaze. 'Would you look at that Aristos, surely it can't be, but it certainly looks like Pegasus flying around looking for a place to land.'

'What's that thing following close behind?' said a confused Aristos, causing Keos to shrug his shoulders.

'Beats me,' said Keos, 'but whatever it is, it's coming into land next to Pegasus'.

Back of the Queue...

The magic case landed gracefully on a patch of land outside the main arena. Fluke and Tash hopped off, stood shoulder to shoulder and whistled when they glanced over at the Olympic stadium.

'Big isn't it,' said Tash glancing nervously at Fluke.

'Just think Tash, we're going to compete in that stadium this afternoon, and with all those thousands of spectators watching I'm beginning to feel a bit nervous.'

Heracles walked over and stood next to Tash, and Bark-at-us padded over and stood next to Fluke, sniffing his tunic hoping to find more dog biscuits.

'Well, looks like we're in time. You'll have to get yourselves registered by joining the other athletes,' Heracles said, pointing to a line entering the stadium.

Appollonia joined them and stood next to Heracles. She was going through a mixture of feelings – happy she had rescued her brother so he could compete in the *diaulos* foot race, but annoyed that officially she couldn't enter herself as girls weren't allowed to compete.

Fluke looked over his shoulder and noticed Heracles whispering to Appollonia and Tash, then he thought he saw Tash open the case, reach inside and pass something to Appollonia. She was nodding and then smiled brightly. Whatever Heracles had said, and whatever Tash had passed her had certainly seemed to cheer Appollonia up.

Turning to her brother and Coroebus, Appollonia said, 'You two join the queue, I'll pop home and tell mum and dad your safe. I'll get a message to your parents as well Coroebus, so I'll pop back and see you later. Oh and I'll take Bark-at-us home as well, mum and dad have been on about getting a new family pet, hope that's OK Fluke?' she waved, and, clutching the item Tash had given her, gave them all a huge grin and hurried off home.

Bark-at-us, with no biscuits being supplied by Fluke, followed Appollonia, barking with joy at the prospect of a new home, and maybe he hoped some biscuits!

'What's she grinning about?' Coroebus said, nudging Demetrios.

'Beats me, she's up to something though,' Demetrios said, shrugged and started to make his way over to the back of the queue. Turning to Fluke and Tash he continued, 'I take it you're competing as well?'

'Of course,' Fluke tugged Tash's paw. 'Come on Tash, we better keep an eye on these two. So tell me Demetrios, will you still speak to us when you finish second behind me or Tash?' joked Fluke.

Tash shook her head and laughed, 'you've done it now Fluke, challenging the two favourites,' and joined the back of the line with the other athletes.

Xene and Heracles walked with them but didn't join the line.

'It's time for me to go home now,' Heracles said looking a little bit sad now the rescue he had helped with was over. 'This adventure has been great fun, even with all those snakes, and it's been great meeting you all, but my dad Zeus has summoned me, apparently he wants me to join someone called Jason and his team of Argonauts, dad tells me they're looking for some magical golden fleece,' he shrugged. 'Guess I'll find out more when I get back home to Mount Olympus.'

Xene said, 'Look, I better get myself home as well. I've got a lot of explaining to do about what dad's been up to, mum is going to furious with him.'

Farewells were exchanged, with Heracles wishing them all the best of luck in the competition. He gave each of them a big hug, mounted Pegasus and flew off, whilst Xene ran home promising to return as soon as she could.

'Well, just the four of us then,' said Tash.

'Yeah, plus several thousand others watching from the stands,' said Fluke peering through the main entrance, the noise levels increasing in volume the closer they got.

Two hours had passed, the line was getting shorter and they were getting closer to the registration desk near the entrance to the magnificent huge arena, when Tash had an idea.

'Fluke, follow me for a second will you,' Tash said, and asked if Demetrios could keep their spot in the line, 'we won't be long,' and she dragged Fluke to a small bush beside them.

'What's up, Tash?'

'We better get changed Fluke,' and opened the magic case. Tash reached inside, took out a new costume, and standing behind the bush got changed. Stepping out from the cover of the bush, Fluke looked her up and down and burst out laughing.

'Well, don't you look the biz,' he chuckled, 'but if you think I'm wearing that you've got to be joking'.

Tash looked at him with one of her stern looks.

'Seriously Tash, I'll look daft. There's thousands of people watching, and they're all going to laugh at us, oh come on, please don't make me wear it,' but Tash wasn't budging, and Fluke finally gave in and agreed to wear the new costume, grumbling all the time as he struggled to get changed.

PE Kit...

Fluke and Tash, now completely changed into their new costumes strode over to Demetrios and Coroebus who were deep in conversation. The pair stopped their talking mid-sentence and looked their companions up and down in surprise.

'What are you two wearing?' said Coroebus, eyeing the two dressed from head to paw in a new outfit.

Bashfully Fluke mumbled, 'Tash has made us wear a PE kit, she seems to think she's suddenly turned into Jessica Ennis.'

'Who's Jessica Ennis?' asked Demetrios.

'Trust me, you won't of heard of her yet. She's an Olympic champion many, many years in your future,' Fluke answered, shaking his head and looking at Tash, who was now wearing running shorts, an athletic vest with her name and number printed on the front, a set of rubber plimsolls on her paws and to complete the outfit she was wearing a sweatband on her head. Fluke was dressed in a similar outfit with his own name and number written in big bold letters on the front of his athletic top.

'Well, if you think it'll help you beat us...' Demetrios shrugged and was then interrupted by a short-haired boy that had appeared and joined them at the back of the queue. He was wearing a PE kit exactly like Fluke and Tash, with a name of Appoll written on the front. Demetrios glanced at the new arrival, smiled and then turned back to speak to Coroebus, both boys confused as to where these new costumes were coming from.

Fluke looked over at the boy, nodded, said hello and asked 'So Appoll, I take it that's your name? Which event are you competing in?' trying to strike up a conversation with the newcomer.

The boy stood closer and whispered, 'So you don't recognise me then?'

Fluke looked closer, frowned and then a huge grin spread over his face as he suddenly realised who the new person was. 'Appollonia?' he whispered, 'what have you done to your hair, it's been cut really short and now I know what Tash passed you earlier, you've got your very own PE kit! But why the name of Appoll?'

'Ssshh' Appollonia said smiling back, 'I've changed my name for the day, had my hair cut to look like Demetrios and am wearing a boy's PE kit that Tash gave me as a disguise.'

Tash joined them and whispered, 'The magic case didn't spell Appollonia correctly, but it's a good thing really as nobody will guess a girl's competing!'

'Let's see how long before my brother recognises that his sister is competing in the Olympics with him!' and the three chuckled to themselves, and watched as Demetrios and Coroebus reached the front of the queue and gave their names and the events they were entering.

Next up was Tash, and she was entering the long jump. Fluke strode up to Aristos and Keos, gave his name and watched as they scribed his name under Tash's on the papyrus and wet clay tablet and confirmed he was entering the javelin. Appollonia – or the newly named Appoll – strode up and put her event down as the discus, her favourite event. Satisfied that nobody had noticed a girl had registered, they all followed Demetrios through into the stadium, and the five of them waited patiently to be introduced to the Hellanodikai, the official judges of the Olympic Games, and be led over to their starting positions.

Lighting the Olympic Flame...

'We're here Tash, we're really, really here at the very first Olympic Games,' said an excited Fluke. 'What an experience, and you never know we might get in the history books by setting a new world record!' said Fluke in awe, gazing around the sights and sounds that surrounded them.

Tash was as spellbound and as excited as Fluke was, totally agreeing that they were lucky to be able to time travel and witness these events, but brought him back down to earth and joked, 'About that world record Fluke, after watching your discus training, do you think they have a world record for the shortest javelin throw?'

'You're soooo not funny Tash, you know I slipped and dropped the discus,' but he did chuckle as he couldn't help but see the funny side. 'Let's just hope that you don't trip up in the long jump in front of so many spectators.'

A huge cheer erupted around the stadium and they looked over to the section where the judges were seated and also where the podium was located for the winners to receive their *kotinos*, an olive wreath that was the prize for the winners at these ancient Olympic Games.

Two burly men were carrying a large fire pit which had been lit in honour of their God Zeus. The Olympic flame was kept alight for the whole day, as the original ancient Games was only a one-day event.

'Did you know the fire pit was lit using the sun's rays?' said Fluke proudly.

'Yes, and all the local temples around Olympia have similar fire pits burning as well,' confirmed Demetrios.

The Tip-Off...

The hooded figure made his way to his seat, confident that today was going to be a good day, although he was blissfully unaware that all his plans were about to change. He made himself comfortable in the stands, waiting like everybody else for the games to start. He ignored the conversations going on around him – the people were excited and were asking each other who they thought was going to win each event.

He chuckled to himself when the conversation came round to the *diaulos* and *stadion* races. Everybody was convinced that Demetrios and Coroebus were the firm favourites and they had both races in the bag, nobody would come near them. *If only they knew that the pair were currently in Tropia under lock and key*, he thought, and allowed himself a contented smile.

A loud voice was calling out the names of the competitors for the first two events. Most of the names meant nothing to him, when suddenly he thought he heard the names Demetrios and Coroebus being called out. He frowned as surely it was a mistake, it couldn't possibly be the same

Demetrios. He stood and glanced down to the starting line and tried to focus on the assembled athletes.

'Excuse me sir, but would you mind following us?' a voice broke his concentration as the *Hood* realised somebody was talking to him. He looked up and noticed a group of large security men had him surrounded.

'Me?' he said, concern and confusion in his voice.

'Yes, you sir,' the head security man said with a lot of authority in his voice. 'If you would please leave quietly as we don't want to make a fuss, now do we?' and the Hood was escorted away from his seat. The guard continued, 'We've had a tip-off from a very reliable source. You've been accused of kidnapping and attempting to fix the events so the favourites don't win.'

Dazed, the *Hood* was led away but as he passed close to the start line he saw to his dismay it *was* Demetrios warming up. The *Hood* broke free from his guards and stormed over to the event organisers shouting, 'Imposter, he's an imposter and not allowed to compete,' causing more than a few heads to turn round and wonder what was happening. Demetrios looked up and saw the hooded figure racing over to him.

Along the side-lines stood Fluke, Tash, Coroebus and Appollonia. She saw what was happening and her instincts kicked in. She picked a smooth round rock and threw it as hard and accurate as possible. The rock sailed through the air and struck the *Hood* squarely in the back causing him to stumble and fall.

Two official judges had witness the spectacular throw. One turned to the other and commented, 'What a *shot*, and it certainly *put* him face down. What do you think about "*The Shot Put*", it could be a great name for a future event,' and scribed some notes for the next Olympic Games.

Appollonia raced over to confront the *Hood*. Heracles had told her earlier he had tipped off the security men, and the *Hood* would be arrested. She grabbed hold of the cloth covering his face and drew it back to identify the kidnapper. 'Otus? Is that really you?' she whispered. Otus was the school sports' instructor, and it now turns out he was also the leader calling himself the Hood holding the secret midnight meetings that Xene's dad used to attend.

'Yes it's me Appollonia, and I would have got away with it too if you and your new friends hadn't interfered,' he indicated Fluke and Tash.

The *Hood* was led away, all the fight had gone out of him. He looked a sorry figure as he realised he had lost all his land on a stupid bet.

That's My Sister...

$\mathcal{D}$emetrios looked over at the events taking place. He'd witnessed the boy that had made friends with Fluke and Tash throw the round rock that struck the *Hood*. Something didn't make sense, something about the technique the boy had used, also the accuracy of the throw... when it suddenly dawned on him, it wasn't a boy after all but his sister in disguise!

'Appollonia?' he whispered, 'I'm sure that's my sister.'

Appollonia couldn't hear her brother, but read his mind. She smiled and gave him a shushing signal by putting her finger to her lips.

What has she done to her hair? He thought, and it suddenly dawned on him. Her conversation with Heracles when they first landed; Tash giving her a costume from the magic case; Appollonia running off home to change and obviously to get mum to cut her hair. The lengths she's gone to just to compete, and he hadn't noticed a thing. He was extremely proud of his little sister, and she deserved to enter and win her event. It made him more determined than ever to make his sister proud of him by winning his own event.

The first ever event of the ancient Olympic Games to take place was Coroebus in the *stadion* race. This was meant to be the highlight of the Games, the opening event. Coroebus looked cool as he stood on the start line and once the race started he flew like the wind around the track leaving everybody way behind to claim the first victory in these new games.

Next up was Demetrios's *diaulos* race. The athletes lined up at the start, all entrants were keen to settle their nerves and get the race started. The starter gave the signal and Demetrios readied himself, looked down the line of competitors and made eye contact with Helios's son, Penthylos who looked back nervously. Demetrios just had to beat him. The race was underway and Penthylos got off to a good start. The noise from the side-lines was deafening, but although there were thousands cheering, Demetrios recognised his sister's, Fluke's and Tash's voices spurring him on. Keeping his cool, Demetrios let his natural ability and fluid running style take over. He powered to the front and claimed a well-deserved victory, winning the event easily.

Several events followed with the athletes soaking up the atmosphere, and then it was Appollonia's turn, the discus event. All of the discus throwers had had their go, and most got some distance. Appollonia looked on and praised her fellow athletes as they came trudging off. She knew a good throw was essential if she was to stand any chance of winning. Appollonia took her place in the *balbis*, the rectangular throwing area, and composed herself. The crowd hushed in respect, and rather than the standard throwing technique everybody else had used, Appollonia used Tash's method of spinning around three times, building up speed and releasing the flat discus at the crucial time. The discus was released from her hand and flew a long way past her nearest competitor. The crowd went wild in celebration as Appollonia realised she was an Olympic champion.

Demetrios ran over and embraced her. 'I knew my little sister would find a way to enter,' he grinned and they hugged each other.

'Well I couldn't let you have all the glory now could I, but I might not have won so easily if that bee hadn't chased Tash around in circles!' she said, giving Tash some credit for developing the new technique, and they all joined in the laughing as Fluke, Tash and Coroebus high-fived each other in celebration.

The congratulations were halted as the last two events were announced. It was now the turn of Fluke and Tash.

The Long Jump...

Their magic case had been left with the judges near the changing area and was safe and sound with everybody else's belongings.

Fluke stood watching Tash go through her warm-up exercises and was trying to give her some words of wisdom, words such as *C'mon you can do it Tash* or *run fast* and the classic that any trainer would be proud of *just jump further than everybody else.*

'Well Tash, Coroebus has won his race, Demetrios has won his and Appollonia, err, I mean Appoll, has won her event as well, so no pressure on us two then!'

'So, remind me Fluke, what did the judge say again, and what am I supposed to do with these?' she gazed at the *halteres*, a pair of items Tash had been given just before she was about to start her run up. These halteres were small hand-held weights or dumbbells that you were meant to hold in each paw, and were designed to allow an athlete to jump a greater distance.

Fluke hurried back to the side-lines whilst Tash paced up and down the track leading to the sandpit swinging her halteres back and forth. She had watched her competitors swing these weights and release them at the last moment and thought it was also about the approach speed. The faster you ran, as long as she got the technique right, the chances were good that the jump should be longer – well that was the plan!

The crowd had been noisy, but again were hushed into a respectable silence as Tash took her place at the start of the long run up. She glanced over to Fluke who had his paws crossed, wishing her luck.

Fluke shouted, 'Just pretend it's a big pile of leaves to leap in, you know how much you love jumping in a big pile of leaves, Tash.'

She tore down the track, the sand getting closer all the time and Fluke's encouraging words actually worked. She did love leaves, in fact adored playing in them. Her pace quickened as she got nearer, and it wasn't sand she saw in front of her, but a huge pile of tempting leaves that was just begging to be jumped in. She hit the spot and released her halters, her paws leaving the ground at exactly the right moment and she sailed through the air and landed to a massive roar from the crowd. She had leapt that far she had nearly jumped over the sand instead of in it.

For a few seconds Tash forgot where she was. She was pretending the sandpit was a huge pile of garden leaves and she began rolling around in it until Fluke ran over to congratulate her. She sat up and was covered head to paw in sand.

'Do you want a bucket and spade Tash to build a sandcastle?' laughed Fluke. 'Just look at you, anybody would think you're on the beach!'

Tash stood up, brushed herself down and, trying not to swallow anymore sand, she asked, 'So how did I do?'

'It was the best jump of the day Tash, and as you're the last one to compete that makes you the champion!'

Tash had won the long jump by a huge margin, and was now being congratulated by the rest. Demetrios and Coroebus shook her paws, and Appollonia gave Tash a big hug.

The celebrations were cut short when the judges called out the names for the final event, the javelin.

The Javelin...

Tash, still buzzing from her massive winning jump, was trying to calm down a nervous Fluke. He was watching the other athletes throw their javelins very long distances. He was watching their techniques very closely and noticed that they threw from a standing position with no run-up at all.

'These boys can certainly throw a long way Tash,' Fluke said, witnessing another long throw.

'You can throw further, Fluke, I know you can. Just believe in yourself and you'll be fine...' Tash said calmly, 'just think, you've helped rescue Demetrios, helped beat the Minotaur, helped beat Medusa, so throwing a wooden stick shouldn't be too much of a problem. Besides, dad is always throwing you a stick to fetch at home and you're always telling me you can throw further than he does!'

Fluke nodded, his confidence growing.

'If you win Fluke, I'll buy you a year's supply of biscuits. If that doesn't encourage you to win, nothing will,' Tash offered.

Tash left him to finish his warm up routine and took her place alongside Appollonia, Demetrios and Coroebus, all watching from the side-lines. Fluke took his javelin from one of the judges, wrapped his paw around and started pacing up and down.

He reached the far end of the track, turned around and began to walk calmly back up to the throw line, when out of nowhere he heard a shout of *behind you Fluke, the Minotaur is loose.* Panic swept through his body and Fluke legged it at full speed down the track wondering how the Minotaur had managed to find him. He didn't see the throw line fast approaching, and he turned to look over his shoulder to see how close the Minotaur's sharp horns were when he tripped. As he began to tumble forward he automatically released his grip on the javelin, his forward body speed was so fast that the javelin shot through the air at an incredible speed and arced gracefully, coming into land a very long way passed his nearest competitor.

Fluke fell into a heap on the ground, waiting for the Minotaur to reach him. A shadow fell over his body and as Fluke looked up he saw Tash standing there, paw outstretched to give Fluke a hand to stand up.

'Where's the Minotaur?' asked Fluke looking all round, dusting himself down.

'There wasn't any Minotaur, Fluke, he's still back in the Labyrinth. It was a joke, I made it up and just shouted out to give you an extra burst of speed, and it worked didn't it...?' She laughed, 'And not wishing to repeat myself from a couple of days ago Fluke, but seriously, did you bring any binoculars with you because you *have* actually thrown it that far I can't see it anywhere; it *must* be a new Olympic record,' and this time Tash really meant it. Fluke had thrown his javelin so far it had easily won him a position on the podium later in the evening to collect his *kotinos*.

Watching the Games...

The stone bowl of magical silvery liquid was balanced carefully on his knees. Zeus was watching all the action unfold and said contentedly, 'I think we can safely say the very first Olympic Games has been very successful. Fluke, Tash, Appollonia, Demetrios and Coroebus have all competed like true champions and they should be proud of themselves, come and take a look,' he smiled and beckoned to his son to come and watch.

Heracles walked over and stood watching over his dad's shoulder. All five of his friends had won the events they entered.

'They certainly have, dad, they've competed really well, although at one point I didn't think they were going to make it back in time. I guess the kidnappers thought they had nearly won, but they didn't bank on Fluke and Tash scuppering their plans.'

'We've got the presentation ceremony coming up and then the final closing ceremony to round off a good day,' Zeus said and was clearly enjoying himself. 'I wish the mortals all over Greece could be here watching these Olympic Games, they'd love them as much as the lucky ones inside the stadium who've been creating a fantastic atmosphere for the athletes to compete in.'

'It's a shame they can't have a magic stone bowl and watch it live like you did,' said Heracles.

'Oh, I know one day the mortals will invent a gadget or device to watch these type of events, and they'll call it a TV or television,' said Zeus settling down to watch the closing ceremony, 'but until then they'll have to read all about it; anyway readings much more fun than watching TV!'

Victory Ceremony...

'The day's been a blur Fluke, so much has happened. I mean this morning we were still rescuing Demetrios,' Tash said, shaking her head, 'and in a couple of hours were going to be on the podium as Olympic champions'.

'Olympic champions Tash, I still can't believe it but it does sound rather good doesn't it!' said Fluke, with a huge grin on his face.

All the competing athletes gathered together to discuss the day's events. They were all excited, each and every one had a huge smile on their faces. Regardless of whether they had won or not, just competing meant everything to them as they all realised they had just taken part in something very special. Coroebus was the outstanding name that everybody was talking about, his winning run made him the very first Olympic champion in history.

The Hellanodikai, official judges for the games, requested the winners make their way over to the temple of Zeus and make themselves ready for the crowning ceremony.

They were cheered by the huge crowds who had stayed behind to witness the victory ceremony. One by one they mounted the steps of the temple, with the carved stone figure of Zeus gazing down.

They were called forward in the order their event had taken place, so up first was Coroebus. His name was read out loud and was then presented with the *kotonis* olive wreath, the branches of which came from the sacred wild-olive tree located near the temple of Zeus. They were cut by a pair of golden scissors, laid in the temple of Hera to be blessed, made into wreaths by the Hellanodikai who then presented them to each winner.

Demetrios was up next, followed by winners from other events including wrestling and chariot racing, when next came the discus.

Fluke, Tash and the rest watched as Appollonia ran up the stone steps. They all had their fingers and paws crossed that none of the judges would notice a girl had not only entered the competition but also won an event. Her name was read out loud, 'Congratulations to Appoll for winning the discus,' said the head judge, 'and not only did you win, but you've also shown us a new throwing style'. Appoll bowed her thanks, and hurriedly left the steps, olive wreath firmly positioned on her head.

'Last up we have two newcomers from a faraway land,' said the head judge, and beckoned Fluke and Tash up the steps to receive their *kotinos*. 'We understand that you have travelled a great distance from the island of Great Britain to join us in these very first Olympic Games, and we congratulate you on winning both the long jump and javelin events.' A huge cheer went up from the crowd as the olive wreaths were placed on the heads of Fluke and Tash.

Fluke, wearing his new olive wreath looked up at the stone statue of Zeus and nudged Tash, 'We've met the real Zeus, Tash, I wonder if he's sat on his huge stone throne watching down on us all from Mount Olympus?' and they both chuckled as they made their way down the steps to be reunited with Coroebus, Demetrios and Appollonia.

'So, who fancies going to the celebration feast tonight?' Appollonia asked. They raised their hands and paws in the air, and she continued, 'Mum and dad are holding a huge party tonight and we're all invited.'

Celebration Feast...

The famous five said their farewells to the other athletes and headed off back to Appollonia and Demetrios house.

As they made their way up the path, the door was flung wide open and a slobbering three-headed dog rushed out to greet them all. Bark-at-us was overjoyed to be reunited with Fluke and Tash and began rolling on the floor, demanding to be stroked and have his belly rubbed.

A steady stream of people came flooding out of the front door. There was Xene and her mum who naturally ran over to Demetrios and Coroebus's parents had been invited who rushed over to embrace their son, and of course Philomela and Herakleitos were as proud as any parent could be as they congratulated the twins.

Philomela gave an extra cuddly hug to both Fluke and Tash and said, 'None of this would have been possible without you two helping to rescue our son.'

'Err, and his little sister might have helped a bit mum!' joked Appollonia laughing, glad things were back to normal 'And he wouldn't be half as good at running or throwing as he is if it wasn't for all that extra training I've put him through.'

'Very true, little sis,' Demetrios smiled. 'You're soooo competitive I really couldn't have won the race if we didn't have our competitions every day before and after school.'

'Let's not forget *the little help*, our gentle giant Heracles! It would have been a lot harder without him,' said Fluke and Tash together, and at that very moment something made everybody look up to the sky. They all saw the huge white stallion Pegasus flying high above with Heracles sat astride. He waved a fond farewell as he was making his way on to a new adventure.

The party started and food was plentiful. Coroebus's mum and dad had brought some of their son's famous bread which was soon devoured by everybody, especially a hungry Fluke and Bark-at-us who both had more than their fair share. Stories were exchanged and jokes made.

Demetrios and Appollonia were back to normal with Appollonia already making plans for the next Olympics, and she stated 'It's only four years until the next Games, we've got plenty of time to train hard to get even better!' to which Demetrios shook his head, laughed, and said, 'Can't we just enjoy this one first Appollonia!'

The evening wore on and before long people began to say their farewells. Coroebus hugged

Fluke and Tash and said he hoped to see them again one day, Xene, who hadn't left Demetrios side all night was eventually persuaded by her mum that it was home time and thanked everybody for a great celebration party.

Fluke and Tash helped Philomela clear up after the party, whilst Demetrios and Appollonia sat talking to their dad, both still buzzing from the day's events. Bedtime was fast approaching and they all trooped off to their rooms for a well earnt night's sleep, with Fluke and Tash sharing the same room as Demetrios and Appollonia.

Within seconds they heard Tash snoring loudly from under the covers. Appollonia smiled to herself, and, remembering their recent adventure, turned to Fluke and said 'Please, no more sleep walking tonight Fluke, I really don't think we could go through all that Labyrinth fiasco again!' and within seconds all their tired bodies drifted off to sleep and joined Tash in a snoring competition.

Morning Sleepy, it's Home Time...

Fluke was having a wonderful dream about winning his javelin event when he was rudely woken by Tash shaking him.

'Wakey, wakey, sleepyhead, its morning and we've got to pack our case.'

'Oh, it's not morning already is it Tash? I was having a lovely dream about winning the javelin.' He slowly opened his bleary eyes, saw his *kotonis* olive wreath by the side of the bed and Tash up and about proudly wearing her *kotonis*. 'So it wasn't a dream Tash, it *was* real, we did actually win!' as yesterday's events all came flooding back. 'We are actual Olympic champions, Tash.' He beamed a huge smile.

'Yeah, well how about becoming an Olympic champion at getting ready for breakfast in double quick time because Philomela is ready to clear away the breakfast table,' and she chuckled and watched as Fluke tore out of bed, got changed and sprinted into the dining area to finish the breakfast laid out before him.

The morning went really quickly as it dawned on Fluke and Tash they were going home today and neither wanted to part company with this lovely family who had made them so welcome.

Tash dragged their magic case outside. Everybody followed and they all stood around waiting for Fluke.

'I forgot my *kotonis*,' he said breathlessly as he tore indoors to retrieve his olive wreath head crown.

Demetrios and Appollonia hugged them both and wished them a safe trip home. 'Don't you forget us now will you,' the twins said with a sad expression, but both were equally extremely happy to have made some great friends.

'You may live hundreds of miles away and many years in the future but side by side or miles apart real friends are always close to the heart, you'll always be our best friends forever and ever,' said Appollonia.

Leaping onto the case Fluke sat behind Tash and watched as she turned the handle three times, the case began to spin and Fluke shouted above the noise, 'Home's that way Tash,' pointing over Tash's shoulder, 'and *pleeeeze,* no olive trees and big purple thundery clouds this time'.

Home Sweet Home...

The magic case appeared out of thin air, skidded along the carpet on the upstairs landing, flew under the ironing board that was always left in an upright position, zipped through the open bedroom door and stopped a few millimetres away from the wardrobe door.

Fluke took a breath and glanced over his shoulder at the digital clock sat on the bedside table, and noticed the time said 12:24. 'Only two minutes have gone Tash since we left, it's just amazing this magic case of ours. Do you think mum and dad would have missed us in two minutes?' he joked.

Tash stepped down onto the carpet, stood and listened to the silent house. 'They don't even know we've been away, Fluke,' she said sniggering to herself. 'Well, another successful adventure Fluke and I must admit an excellent choice of yours,' she said, patting him on the back. They both changed out of their costumes, opened the case and threw them inside.

'What's that there?' asked Fluke as he spied a clay pot in the bottom of the case.

Tash retrieved the clay pot and laughed. 'Looks like a present from Demetrios and Appollonia – it's a clay pot full of Herakleitos home-pressed olive oil,' she said, sniffing the contents of the pot. 'We'll have some later with our dinner,' and turned to store their case back in the back of the wardrobe.

Padding downstairs they entered the kitchen. Tash leapt up onto the work surface and Fluke handed her the clay pot which Tash stored in the back of the overhead cupboard. 'Won't mum and dad be surprised when they see this,' Tash chuckled, closing the cupboard door.

'They'll never guess where it came from,' laughed Fluke, and the pair made their way back up the long flight of stairs and tiptoed passed mum and dad's bedroom door, onto the landing, and made their way to the spare bedroom.

Tash leapt up onto the sofa and watched as Fluke went over to the computer. 'What are you doing Fluke?' she asked in fascination, as he turned on dad's computer.

'Just checking something Tash,' he mumbled as the computer screen blinked into life, casting a glow around the bedroom.

He tapped away on the keyboard and beckoned Tash to come and see what he had found. 'It's the internet Tash, and I've looked up the Olympic Games, 776 BC, look what it says "*Coroebus of Elis, commonly spelled Koroibos, was a humble*

Greek cook, baker and an athlete from Elis, he won the stadion race in the first recorded Ancient Olympic Games in 776 BC"'.

Fluke scrolled down a bit further and found another line, *"The prize he received was an olive branch, though the honour of winning was far more prestigious than the actual prize"*. Fluke was about to turn off the computer when Tash asked, 'Anything about us competing? Did we get our names mentioned?' she asked excitedly.

Fluke scrolled down a bit more but shook his head. 'All it says is *"The complete number of sports that were carried out in each of the Games is unknown, as is the number of victors that took part in these."'* and he shrugged as he turned off the computer screen.

'I guess it's probably for the best that nobody knows we competed, it may be a bit complicated trying to explain that to mum and dad if they ever found out where we've been!' laughed Tash and went back to her favourite position on the sofa.

Dinosaur Adventure...

Fluke snuggled up on the sofa, but he and Tash were unable to sleep as they were still too excited about their recent adventure.

'Where to next, Tash?' Fluke asked. 'It'll have to be a good adventure to come close to Ancient Greece. How far back in time do you think the magic case can actually travel?'

Tash thought about this last comment and scratched her head, 'Do you know what Fluke, I really don't, never even thought about it, but next time how about putting the magic case to the test and see how far back we can travel?'

'Wow, yes let's see,' he said breathlessly.

'What about the dinosaurs?' Tash looked over at Fluke and heard him gulp.

'What, like big creatures with sharp claws and very sharp teeth?' he asked, thinking Tash was joking.

'Yes Fluke, but they had all sorts of dinosaurs. Some big, some small, you might even get a dinosaur that's afraid of you!' she giggled. 'We might find some Brontosaurus, Stegosaurus...' Fluke interrupted and chipped in with some suggestions of his own, '*Do-you-think-he-saw-us*, or maybe a *silly-a-saw-us*'. Fluke was chuckling at his made-up names.

They yawned and agreed to start planning their next adventure in the morning, drifting off and both dreaming of dinosaurs.

A Glossary of Greek words and their English meanings:

Balbis – A rectangular area for athletes was used in the Olympic Games as a throwing area. Competitors couldn't step out of the balbis or they would be disqualified.

Diaulos – An ancient Greek unit of measurement approximately 370 metres.

Dolichos – An ancient Greek unit of measurement. 25 Dolichos is approximately 50 kilometres, or a whole day trip on a horse and cart.

Hellanodikai – The official judges of the ancient Olympic Games.

Heracles – His official name was spelt Heracles, it was only later that the Romans changed the spelling to Hercules.

Kotinos – The olive wreath was the prize for a winner at the ancient Olympic Games. It was a branch of the wild olive tree that grew at Olympia, intertwined to form a circle or a horseshoe.

Olympiad – A period of four years between each Olympic Games, used by the ancient Greeks in dating events.

Stadion – An ancient Greek unit of measurement which is approximately 190 metres long, which is nearly the same as the 200 metres race in our modern Olympic Games.